ALPHA TURNED

WOLF APPEAL BOOK 1

KB ALAN

ABOUT THIS BOOK

Alpha Turned

Not all men are bad...

Strong, independent, and happy on her own, Hillary has grown from the naïve person she was four years ago after a brutal rape turned her into a werewolf. The normal life she's made for herself is only upset once a month when the moon calls to her and she has an uncontrollable urge to turn furry and chase small creatures. And she doesn't need a man for that. Until she finally meets another werewolf, this one a gorgeous, sexy guy who is determined to change her mind about one furry man in particular–him.

No, some men are very, very good...

The minute Zach scents Hillary he knows she's the mate he's been searching for. Though both the wolf and the man are itching to claim her, first he has to convince her that he's one of the good guys, and that there are certain benefits to being an alpha werewolf. And there's no better way of making Hillary see that, than giving her himself—body, mind, and soul.

CHAPTER ONE

Hillary was not a happy camper.

Meeting new people always made her nervous, but here she was on her way to meet her boyfriend's family. Being in a relationship with Jeff for the past four months had helped her get over her aversion to strangers, somewhat. He not only boosted her confidence but occasionally managed to drag her out to parties and other social occasions that she otherwise would have ignored. And sometimes, she had fun. If she didn't, chances were he didn't either, and they could leave to do something else. Somehow she didn't think that would work quite so well when it came to a three-day spring break visit with his family.

Her lapse into silence must have signaled her worry to Jeff because he reached over and took her hand. "Don't be nervous, hon. They'll love you."

She flashed him a smile, appreciating that he'd known what was wrong.

"I'm sure they're great, I'm just not used to big families." Massive understatement.

"I know when your parents died, you lived with guardians. Didn't you have any other family to go to?" Sympathy and understanding didn't quite drown out his obvious disbelief that such a thing was possible.

She shifted in her seat. It wasn't something she liked to think about often, let alone talk about. But one of the reasons—actually, the main reason—that she'd agreed to the road trip was so that they could get to know each other better. The six hours of driving time between their college in Los Angeles and his family in Phoenix had seemed perfect.

"Well, my mom's grandparents were in a nursing facility. My dad has a brother on the East Coast somewhere, but they weren't in touch."

He gave her hand a squeeze and changed the subject to tell her a funny story about the song playing on the radio. That was one of the things she liked about him. He was careful not to push her too much. She'd taken things very slowly, reluctant to let a relationship distract her from her studies. While she had some money from her parents' estate, her scholarship was very important to her and she had made school her number one priority. She'd been very clear about that to Jeff when he'd first started asking her out.

Only once had he pushed for more than she was ready to give. When she'd suggested that they break up he'd immediately backed down, never again pushing when she said she didn't have time for what he was suggesting. In return, she'd tried to be careful not to use that as an excuse to put off going out, when she really only wanted to stay in. She'd come to recognize that isolating herself from other people was a defense mechanism that she needed to get over.

When he'd asked her to join him for this trip, she'd known he was hoping that by its end she would feel comfortable enough to finally sleep with him. A big part of her hoped that he was right. She was nervous about it. He would be her first and she really hadn't been ready to take that step before. But things had been getting hot and heavy between them and she was at the point that she wanted more.

"So your parents will be there, and your uncle, you said. Any cousins?"

"No cousins yet. Uncle Ken is single." He sounded pleased that she was asking. "But there's other extended family and they have kids, so there are always some rug rats running around." He slanted her a quick look that she couldn't read.

"Do you ever think about having kids?" he asked carefully.

Had she made it so hard for him to talk to her about real issues that he was afraid to ask her questions?

"Sure, in an indefinite, theoretical, far-in-the-future sort of way. I guess I just always assumed that I would, when the time was right. You're an only child too. Would you want to have more than one?"

The fact that she answered and didn't snap at him seemed to relax him. Wow, maybe she really had been way too hesitant to discuss personal matters. Sometimes she wondered why he'd put up with her for this long.

"I think I'd like a large family. You're right, though, it seems so far in the future. Right now it's hard to imagine what will happen after I graduate next year."

They pulled off the freeway and headed away from the city. Jeff got her talking about a class she was looking forward to taking next semester with her favorite professor, distracting her enough that she was only a little bit nervous as they made their way down a long driveway.

She took a deep breath and looked around. Ahead of them and to the right was a large ranch-style house. There was a cluster of smaller homes past Jeff's window. People began walking toward the main house as they drove past, seeming to have headed over at the arrival of their car.

"Oh good, looks like everyone is coming over, probably for a barbecue," Jeff said, opening his door.

"Great," Hillary muttered softly, plastering a smile on her face. She wouldn't even get to meet the parents first before the rest of the family. She got out and moved to the back to get her things. Glancing over her shoulder, she saw three people rounding the corner of the house, Jeff heading toward them. She shouldered her backpack and made her way toward the group, pleased when Jeff stopped to take her hand before leading her to the others.

"Mom, Dad, Uncle Ken, this is Hillary Abbott. Honey, these are my parents John and Shannon Cage, and my uncle Ken Cage." He smiled proudly and she blushed.

Hillary put her hand out but Shannon Cage grabbed her up in a hug.

"We are so glad to meet you! Jeff has told us how special you are and we can't wait to get to know you," the woman squealed.

Hillary glanced up at John and Ken Cage. John was smiling as broadly as his wife, and sending a satisfied look toward his son. Ken looked...condescending? Hillary wondered. Maybe calculating? Whatever was going on there, she didn't care for it. She backed out of Shannon's embrace and shrugged the backpack higher up on her shoulder. Shannon took the hint.

"Let's get you and your things to your room. You'll want to freshen up after that long drive. Dinner will be ready soon and then we'll have the bonfire."

Jeff seemed a little surprised by that. "We're having a bonfire tonight, Mom? Shouldn't we wait a couple of days?"

They began moving toward the front door.

"Nonsense. We want to be able to enjoy as many days as possible with both you kids before you have to drive back to school."

Hillary didn't really see what that had to do with anything, but decided she didn't particularly care, either. She wasn't too surprised that she didn't immediately like Jeff's family. Quite frankly she didn't immediately like anyone, but she was a little bit worried about how uneasy she felt. Unlike the parties they attended together at school, she couldn't expect Jeff to agree with her that it would be more fun to leave early and go off to do their own thing. This time she was just going to have to suck it up.

Besides, two minutes with three people didn't mean that she couldn't have a good time. There must be twenty people milling around, so chances were she'd like at least some of them. Jeff stopped in front of a door and opened it for her. She gave him a kiss and a smile.

"I'll just freshen up a bit. Fifteen minutes?"

"I'm glad you came. I think, after the bonfire, we'll be closer than ever." He leaned in and gave her a soft kiss.

She willed her tension to drain away. "I'll be right out."

The look of excitement on his face made her smile as she closed the door. Making him happy would make her happy. She'd been awfully selfish in their relationship. It was time to make a little bit of effort for him.

It took only a few minutes to wash her face, brush her hair back into a neat ponytail and reapply a bit of makeup. She stared at her reflection and tried out a welcoming smile. Not exactly Miss Mary Sunshine, but not terrible, either. It wasn't as though she had to become best friends with these people. The three days would fly by and then they would be home.

The sun was going down but it was still warm outside so she changed into a clean pair of shorts and a tank top. Practicing the smile once more, she headed for the door.

THE NEXT FEW hours were unsettling. She met many people and most of them were nice to her. A few were even too nice. She wasn't sure what it was about them as a group that was making her so uncomfortable. Some of the family treated her as if she were Jeff's fiancée, rather than a relatively new girlfriend. She'd swear many of them had been sniffing her, which made her especially uncomfortable since she'd been sitting in a car for six hours before meeting them.

There seemed to be a larger percentage of creepy guys and bitchy girls than she thought was normal for a group this size. Jeff's mom insisted on dragging her around and cheerfully introducing her until she'd officially met every single person present.

It just couldn't be normal to be that cheerful all the time, Hillary thought as she finally managed to escape the slightly mad woman. Jeff was sitting on a log near the fire pit. She sat down beside him and put her head on his shoulder, needing to feel as if someone there liked her for herself. She would sit with him for a few minutes, then tell him she was tired and excuse herself to bed.

Jeff put his arm around her and she closed her eyes, enjoying the familiar comfort. After a while she realized it had gone quiet. She opened her eyes and lifted her head. People were quietly coming to the fire pit area and sitting down, ending their conversations. Hillary realized the children were all gone now and figured that was a good sign that it was late enough for her to excuse herself. Ken, Jeff's uncle, was the only one left standing, and everyone was looking at him expectantly.

"As you all know, Jeff has brought a guest today, his girlfriend Hillary, to introduce her to us. You've all had a chance to meet her, talk to her and form your own opinions. Jeff has asked permission to mate, and I've decided that the female is acceptable."

There was a low murmur of approval, some sniffs of disapproval. Hillary wondered if she had fallen asleep. Otherwise this group was even more insane than she'd first thought. She tensed, and Jeff's arm around her waist tightened. He straightened his spine, and she waited to hear what he had to say to this ridiculousness.

"Thank you, Alpha. I am honored that you have approved my first choice." He bowed his head for a moment. Hillary, looking at him as if he were crazy, realized that the odd gleam in his eye might in fact mean that he *was* crazy. She rose, but he rose with her, squeezing her to his side.

Ken spoke again. "It will remain to be seen if she is your mate, as you believe. Once she's taken the bite, you and I will know for sure. If so, we will all be pleased for you."

Hillary looked around, expecting to see at least some of the people laughing at the show, but everyone was looking very seriously at either her or the freak speaking.

"However," Ken continued, "as you know, if she is not your mate after all, you will allow the hierarchy their chance to discover if she is one of theirs before you marry, if that is still your wish."

Jeff bowed his head again, "Of course, Alpha."

The conversation was so bizarre that Hillary wasn't sure how to react. She *was* sure that she didn't want Jeff holding her anymore. She elbowed him in the ribs and stepped back when his arm jerked free. Some of the men laughed, and she distinctly heard "feisty", "bitch" and "uppity" from the crowd. Hillary decided enough was enough and turned to leave.

Deep growls stopped her midstride. She turned back around just in time to see three of the men turn into wolves. *Holy shit.* Anger turned to terror in a heartbeat. Ken, who was staring right at her, held up his hand. All eyes were on him as Hillary began backing away. Ken's arm dropped, the wolves howled and all hell broke loose. She turned and ran toward the house, knowing she had to get behind a locked door before the pack of wolves got to her.

She didn't make it. What felt like a ton of bricks landed on her back. She hit the ground hard, barely getting her hands up in time to save her face from hitting first. There were growls and snarls, teeth and nails and slobber, as she fought, screamed, kicked and cursed. Finally, she found herself on her back, being held down, a man at her wrists, above her head, a woman on one leg, a wolf on the other. But it was the thing on top of her, clearly Jeff but part wolf, his face distorted into a muzzle baring sharp teeth, his very hairy arms ending in clawed hands, that convinced her that she was living a true nightmare.

"She's all yours, Jeff," the man holding her arms said to the creature snarling in her face. "At least for now."

Hillary looked into the beast's eyes and the fact that they were Jeff's was almost more than she could comprehend. She didn't believe in witches or fairies, vampires or werewolves. While her mind prayed that this was the most bizarre and vivid nightmare she'd ever had, her body struggled for freedom. Her eyes flicked right and left and she realized that she was surrounded by at least a dozen wolves. She bucked upward, trying desperately to free some part of her body, just as Jeff's jaws opened and descended on her neck.

The pain was incredible for a long time as she swam in and out of consciousness. Her whole body was screaming. She tried to concentrate but it was too much and she was swallowed back down into the darkness. At some point she became aware of being on a bed and realized that Jeff had woken her up. He was trying to thrust his fingers into her dry passage as he began to kiss her.

Was it better, or worse, that he was back to his old self, the Jeff who she'd thought she was coming to love instead of the monster that had attacked her? She turned her head but the pain from her neck wound was incredible. She tried to hit him, but her arms were tied down. He bit her neck, hard, on the side that wasn't already wounded. He grabbed her hair and forced her lips to his. She kept her mouth closed and he yanked until she gasped then plunged his tongue in deep. She bit him and he jerked back and slapped her face. She nearly passed out again, and wished that she had when he forced his cock into her.

It felt as if she was being ripped apart and she tried to struggle, but her legs were tied down as well as her arms. She didn't cry until she realized what he was saying, over and over, as he thrust into her passage, now slick with blood. "I love you, I love you, I love you..." She gave up, letting the darkness take her.

HILLARY WOKE up feeling as if she were dying of thirst. Instead of being tied to a bed, she was on a mattress lying on a concrete floor, in a windowless room. It smelled damp and contained the mattress, a toilet and a sink. There was a rough bandage taped to her neck.

Crawling to the sink, she hoisted herself up far enough to drink some water. She used the toilet then tested the door. Locked and probably even sturdier than it looked. She sat down on the floor next to the door, her back to the wall. The mattress smelled of her rape and she was dimly aware that she'd been in this room for a couple of days, long enough for at least three men that she could remember to come in and take their turn. She also remembered Jeff raping her again, enraged, screaming, "You were supposed to be my mate. Why aren't you my mate?" She barely made it back to the toilet before she vomited.

On the fourth day, when they came to get her, she was so weak she could barely even think about escaping, let alone act on it. She hadn't eaten since the barbecue, had only water from the sink. Two men, possibly Jeff and his father—she was simply too weak to notice —came to drag her from the room. She cried out faintly as the wound in her neck throbbed at the movement.

They brought her outside and dumped her on the ground. Hillary was vaguely aware that she was surrounded by many people. The moon was shining brightly enough for her to see that they weren't really paying much attention to her. Everyone was stripping out of their clothes and holding their faces up to the moon. Her body began to tingle and her battered mind wondered if what had already happened wasn't the worst to come.

It took only a moment before she was once again surrounded by wolves. Some of them came to her where she was lying on the ground trying desperately to figure out what she should be doing, how she could escape these monsters. They began to nip at her and nudge her—and not in a playful way. She ignored them and concentrated on the feeling that was filling her up inside. Somehow she knew it was the moonlight, that it was warming her up when she hadn't even realized she was cold.

Part of her recognized that it felt good and powerful, but the other part of her was so exhausted and terrified and *angry* that she resisted its pull for as long as she could. The wolves grew tired of watching her and took off, yipping and howling.

In and out of consciousness, Hillary heard them, running and playing, grunting and fucking. The warmth and tingling were nearly overpowering her, making her body tremble. The wolves became human again, going past her into the house in small groups. Some of them stopped to kick at her.

"What a waste. Too weak to be one of the chosen," a male voice said.

"She didn't even turn. She won't make it through the night." The woman sounded young and pleased.

"Damn, I wish I could have had her again before we have to bury her."

She was sweating with the effort of holding back whatever it was that was happening to her when she heard Jeff's voice.

"I guess all that toughness was just an act. Stupid bitch."

Hillary used the disgust and anger his words caused to hold on, to be stronger. Finally, when she hadn't heard anyone for more than an hour, Hillary at last gave in to the feeling, let the power of the moon wash through her. She realized that she hurt less at about the same time she realized she was seeing in black and white. She stumbled to her feet—all four of them.

CHAPTER TWO

The music was blaring at Larry's Woodworking shop, Korn spitting out a sharp, fast beat for the early morning hour. Todd, the realtor who'd found the location for her, had given her the nickname. It made her roll her eyes but it had stuck and been the obvious choice when it came time to name the shop.

Slade had been the next town on her list of possibilities with nothing to recommend it to her other than its remoteness. Her intention was to find a quiet place, free of wolves, where she would be left alone. She would open a cabinetry shop to make money until she could make a reputation for the custom woodworking she loved.

Todd had been the only real estate agent, taking her around town, telling her about the businesses that were already there. He'd assured her that there was no direct competition for what she wanted to do. Despite her intention to remain a loner, he and his wife had somehow become her best friends.

After about a year she'd stopped the cabinetry work. Six months later she'd needed to hire an assistant and was still having to turn away some business. Today she was working on a bed for the town mayor, a surprise for his wife. It would be beautiful, she thought.

Cherry wood, hand-carved, four posters. Mayor Davies had come in without any real specifics on what he wanted, just some pictures of how his wife had decorated their home, especially the bedroom.

Hillary had sketched out a couple of possibilities, and he'd given her free rein with the one he thought Darla would like best. She'd met the mayor and his wife that first weekend she had scouted the area. After touring the town with Todd she'd told him she was going to sniff around on her own for the rest of the weekend and would be in contact with him afterward. Of course, he hadn't realized that she had meant that literally .

The first town on her list of possibilities had also looked like a good prospect from a business standpoint, and she hadn't detected anything resembling a werewolf there, but the next town up the highway, she'd smelled at least two. The towns were only eight miles apart so she hadn't even bothered to get out of her car, had just kept on going.

The second place on her list hadn't suited her from a business standpoint, which had brought her to Slade. True to her word, she'd spent the weekend literally sniffing out the small town, then all of the neighboring ones to ensure that there were no werewolves she could discover.

She hadn't seen a werewolf since that night when she'd escaped the lunatics in Arizona. Afraid to go back to L.A., she'd made her way to Dallas. There she'd recuperated, not so much physically as that had happened astonishingly quickly, but mentally. Returning to college just hadn't seemed attractive. Instead she'd found herself doing something she never would have guessed at, turning the hobby she'd shared with her father into a business. Woodworking had been a comfort, not a business plan, but she'd embraced its familiarity and the sense of peace it brought her after the trauma of Arizona. It had taken a couple of false starts to find someone she could work with and learn from while maintaining an emotional distance, but she'd managed it until she felt comfortable going out on her own.

A couple of times in Texas she'd smelled the distinctive scent of

werewolves, but had kept well clear. After the third time, when she had been in an area of the city she wasn't very familiar with and therefore not totally sure of the best way to avoid contact, she'd decided to find a place that suited her needs better.

Her three years in Slade had not made her careless. She was still constantly on guard. She went into the surrounding mountain forests often as a human, but had only encountered natural wolves, who smelled very different and shied away from her no matter what form she was in.

Every couple of months, when the moon was at its darkest, she would let her wolf come out. It was difficult, a struggle sometimes to ignore the pull, especially when the moon was full and bright. She wasn't even sure anymore why she resisted, but she was stubborn like that, and just contrary enough to ensure that she was only letting the wolf out when *she* wanted to.

Well, that wasn't exactly true, she would just as soon never make the change, but she couldn't deny any longer that she did get a great deal of enjoyment those brief days when she let the wolf out to play. Todd worried about her on those weekends that she insisted on going "camping" alone, but she told him she had her cell phone and wouldn't wander into areas where there wasn't coverage. She didn't like lying to him and did so as rarely as possible, but it was more important to her that she be far away from people when she let the wolf out.

When the phone rang, Hillary debated answering it before reaching up and pausing the CD player. Her assistant was out getting some supplies. She gave a small sigh then squared her shoulders and answered the phone. "Larry's Woodworking, can I help you?"

"Yes, my name is Aaron Jenner, I've been working with Stephen on a custom quote for a dining table."

"Yes, Mr. Jenner. I believe Stephen faxed a drawing to you." Hillary instantly brought to mind the quote that Jenner was talking about, a table she was looking forward to working on if the quote was accepted.

"Right, I got the drawing and I think it looks great, but since I don't know much about tables, and since I'm going to be in your area tomorrow, I thought it would be a good idea to come by and speak with whoever I need to, face-to-face, just to be sure we're all on the same page." He sounded apologetic. "The truth is the drawing is nice and all, but I just don't know how it will look in 3D, if you get my meaning." He laughed lightly at himself.

Hillary smiled. She was constantly amazed at how many non-designers tried to have something custom built without really admitting that they knew nothing about design or construction, and therefore couldn't really be sure what they would be getting. It was her job, and one she was training Stephen on, to make sure that they were making what the customer wanted, not just what they asked for.

"Of course, Mr. Jenner. What time will you be in the area? Stephen and I should both be around most of the day and we can pause whatever we're working on to discuss the table design with you."

"Great." He sounded relieved. "I thought this was a great idea for a gift until Stephen asked me specifically what I wanted." He laughed again. "I should be there around two o'clock, but I can bum around for a bit if there's a better time for you."

"Two o'clock is not a problem. We'll be ready for you."

Hillary hung up the phone, turned the stereo back on and got back to work. When Stephen came back to the shop, she let him turn the player down and listened to him recount the shopping expedition. Satisfied that he'd gotten everything they needed, and curious about a couple of things he thought she might like, she brushed off her apron and stretched.

"Aaron Jenner called. He said that he got the drawing, but since he's going to be in the area he figured it would be easiest to stop by and talk to us about the design. Tell me again exactly what he asked for when you first spoke?"

They walked to her office and Stephen sat down on the couch as she fetched sodas for both of them before sitting in the large leather chair behind her desk.

"He said he wanted to have a huge medieval-style dining table made for his brother. Something you would find in a castle, not fancy but rough and warrior-ish." Stephen took a drink from the can then winked. "He sounded nice and warrior-ish himself. Kind of growly, dontcha think?"

Hillary laughed and quirked an eyebrow at him. "Do I need to give you a lecture about coming on to our clients before he gets here tomorrow?" she asked. She pulled out the drawing, although she already knew what was on it. "Well, I think you have here what he asked for. He's just having a hard time seeing it on paper. Get that leftover piece of wood from the Turners' cabinet, distress the hell out of it and see how much of a finish you can get on it before he gets here. We'll give him something he can see so he knows that we know what he wants."

"Will do," Stephen said, pushing up off the sofa. He paused in the doorway and looked back at her. "What exactly *is* the rule about coming on to clients?"

Hillary picked a paperclip up off her desk and threw it at his retreating back.

THE NEXT DAY, Hillary and Stephen had moved from the shop to her office after lunch, going over some designs for other customers. When they heard the outer door open, Stephen got up to show their client in to her office. She stood up and walked around the desk to greet him as they came through the door. "Mr. Jenner, this is Hillary Abbott, otherwise known as Larry. Hillary, this is Mr. Jen... I'm sorry, do you two know each other?" Stephen asked, confused.

As soon as they'd reached the doorway, Hillary had scented werewolf. Fear and anger barreled through her at an astonishing rate. Before Stephen had even said her name her breath was coming in short spurts, her eyes had gone huge, and her body was edging toward Stephen to protect him from the werewolf.

Her eyes never left the man's face, so she saw his nose quiver as he registered her scent, his lips smile as he realized what she was, and his eyebrows go up as he noticed her response. He blinked, darted a look at Stephen, then stepped back slightly so he was on the other side of the doorway, turning to the side so that he wasn't blocking the exit.

"Uh...yes, sort of. Listen, Stephen, do me a favor and go—" Hillary, her eyes still locked to Jenner's face, faltered in the excuse, "away. I'll call you later. Don't come back until then."

Stephen started to laugh then stopped. "Right. Okay, whatever you say, boss. Are you sure? I could stay in the shop or something."

"No, it's fine, I'll call you. Thanks." Hillary took his arm and walked him past Jenner, squeezing through the door with him so that she was between the two men. Jenner stepped back further, giving them more room. He stayed put as she followed Stephen to the door. Hillary's heart was pounding and the blood was rushing through her ears. She couldn't think!

She stood at the door until she saw Stephen's car pull out, her ears trained behind her for any sound of movement. She turned around. Jenner stood where he'd been, his hands out slightly in a gesture of harmlessness. He opened his mouth to say something, but then closed it.

Fear coursed through her, which just pissed her off. She knew that he could smell her fear, which made her even angrier. She heard a low growling sound and was astonished to realize it was coming from her own throat. She whirled around and stalked outside. She went toward the strange truck in the parking lot, smelling what she thought she would—this wolf, but others as well. She moved over to her own car and leaned against it.

"What are you doing here?" she finally asked, as he followed her lead and stood against his truck.

"I came to get a table made for my brother. We didn't know you were here. How come you haven't checked in with the alpha? You've obviously been here for some time." He kept his voice low, carefully unthreatening, but the suspicion was there.

Hillary looked around. There were other businesses adjoining hers, other people out and about. "I'm not going to talk about this here. Go away."

Jenner stared at her for a moment, looked around then nodded his head. "One hour." He got in his truck and drove back toward the highway.

Hillary popped the trunk on her car and pulled out a backpack. She went back into the office and changed into the sweatpants and t-shirt that were inside, as well as the jogging shoes. She put her car key in the special pocket of the shoes, locked up the shop and deposited the bag and her purse back into the trunk. She kept her cell phone in her hand as she started to jog.

It only took her twenty minutes to get all the way outside town, into the forest to a little-used campground. There were other camp-grounds more conveniently situated that the locals used, so Hillary had taken to using this one as a starting-off point for her trips into the deeper woods. She sat down on a long, wide log situated in front of the blackened fire pit. She took off her jogging shoes and socks, sticking her cell phone inside one of the shoes and the socks in the other, and tucked them next to the log. If she had to change—to fight—she was prepared.

She worked to calm herself. Jenner hadn't seemed angry to have found an unexpected werewolf, more surprised. He hadn't given off a single threatening vibe, but had been suspicious. As though he'd found her doing something she wasn't supposed to be doing. Really, though, what did she know? She hadn't found Jeff or his family to be threatening. They'd just been annoying, until the moment they'd attacked her.

She thought about the life she'd built in Slade—the business, the friends, the sense of community. She wasn't about to give that up if she didn't have to. She would fight to keep what she'd made. She was strong, damn it. She could and would protect her friends, her town. If she was a bit nervous, it wasn't that much more than when she went off to the woods to change. It always frightened her to give in to the power that was constantly running through her veins, waiting for an outlet. This time, if she needed to, it wouldn't frighten her. She would revel in her strength, her power.

Raising her face to the sky, Hillary breathed in the piney scents, the nearby animals, the river a mile off, the cars on the highway. She let herself feel the wolf inside, gave it a nudge, felt the power that had been stirring since her fear and anger had hit her, solidify, waiting for her to let it free. This was one of the reasons she denied the change as often as possible. The truth was, once she let it free, it felt glorious. Part of her, a huge part of her, feared giving in to the seductiveness of that power.

Jenner's approach was not noisy but not silent either. Hillary gave him credit for making sure that she knew he was there. He stopped on the far side of the old campfire and watched her. He seemed more suspicious than before, but still not angry or dangerous. He took in her changed clothes, and she saw that he had untucked his shirt, removed his belt and untied his boots. The wedding ring he'd been wearing earlier was gone. They were both ready to change if necessary.

Finally he broke the silence. "I checked in with the alpha. He's unaware of werewolves living in this town. You've broken national law."

Hillary's right eyebrow cocked in surprise. "There's a national law?" she asked, before she could stop herself.

His nostrils flared and he took a step closer. "You're not part of a pack," he stated, as if confirming something.

"No."

"You've *never* been part of a pack?" He growled, but she didn't feel threatened.

"No."

He walked to the other end of the log she was sitting on. "There's an old werewolf fairy tale about a woman getting pregnant and not knowing the man was a wolf until her kid changes. I think it's supposed to remind bratty children that they should be happy they get to be raised in a pack."

"No. Nothing from a fairy tale."

He smiled for a second but it quickly fell away. She turned her head to face him, resting her chin on her fist, her elbow on her knee. She knew he believed her, could smell her emotions and the truth of what she was saying. She was no longer scared but her heart rate increased as he worked his way around to the truth.

"No." This time he was the one to say it. She looked away, facing forward again, so that she could just see him out of the corner of her eye. His face had gone pale. "No, it doesn't happen anymore."

"No?"

"No, damn it, no!" He thrust to his feet. Hillary stood too in reflex, but he didn't come any nearer. He lowered his head. "Tell me."

She thought about it. She didn't know why, but she liked this man. There was something sweetly appealing about him. He clearly wasn't a weak man and would most definitely not be a weak wolf, but she didn't fear him. That didn't mean she didn't fear what he represented, but she couldn't judge that adequately until she found out more. She wouldn't find out more without talking to him. Of course, she'd made mistakes about people in the past, but at least this time she knew she could defend herself if necessary.

"My college boyfriend took me home to meet the family. They attacked me, raped me, and left me for dead. I managed to get away and have never spoken to another werewolf."

Jenner's chest heaved and sweat beaded his forehead. He ran his hands through his hair. Hillary could just barely make out his muttering, "Shit, shit, shit." She could smell his fury and disgust. Inside she felt the power trying to take hold, the wolf wanting to defend or attack, but she pushed it away. He didn't look at her, but toed off his boots.

"I'm sorry, I need to go...kill something. I'll be back." He jogged into the trees, and she heard the rustling as he took off his jeans and t-shirt then a long, mournful howl.

She sat down on the ground, her back against the log, her head resting on her knees. Over the years she had been curious about other werewolves. She'd wondered if they would be the same, or if the Cages were just a special kind of crazy. On the one hand, what were the chances that she would fall in not just with werewolves, but with crazy werewolves? On the other hand, they had most definitely been crazy, so why assume there couldn't be sane werewolves?

She'd decided the issue wasn't worth investigating. It was too dangerous. Besides, she'd spent the last four years denying the wolf inside herself as much as possible, so what would be the point in meeting others? Something about the way Jenner had asked about being part of a pack, though, had resonated with her. He had seemed as if it were the most natural thing in the world. As if it were family.

It had been a long time since Hillary had been part of a family. As nice as it might sound, she was sure she was too set in her ways at this point to be willing to make the compromises that were necessary in a family environment. No, it was crazy. She would tell these people, this Aaron Jenner and his alpha, whatever that meant, that she hadn't asked for this, didn't know their laws, and they could just leave her to her little town. She would listen to any requests they had to make about laws she should follow, and if they were reasonable she would assure them of her compliance. Other than that, they could kiss her ass.

When the wolf approached, Hillary looked up and caught her breath. He was beautiful, brown and gold, huge and soft. He waited until she was looking at him, and then moved slowly toward her, watching her body, judging her response, but not looking her in the eyes. Hillary lowered her knees and put her hands on her thighs. He came up to her outstretched legs, his body close to the ground, and whined.

Hillary spread her legs a bit so that he could come closer, and reached her hand out to touch that beautiful fur. He bellied between her legs, darting his eyes up to check her face, then rolled over onto his back, resting his head on her thigh so that his neck was showing. She swallowed hard, her throat choking up and her eyes getting hot, and rubbed his belly.

She scratched deep with her nails then rubbed his neck softly. He rumbled in pleasure, licked her hand, and rolled to his side, cradled in her lap, his head on her thigh. He closed his eyes and relaxed. Hillary kept petting him, leaning back against the log, until the tears came. Then she tugged on his ruff until he was sitting, buried her face in his fur and started crying. In four years she'd never cried, and now she sobbed. She wrapped her arms around the big wolf, letting him lick gently at whatever part of her he could reach, soaking up the comfort he offered just with his presence.

CHAPTER THREE

Zach answered the phone as he placed his dinner on the table. He'd been waiting for his brother to call him back and update him on the situation with an unknown wolf in their territory. The chances were slim that it was anything serious, but he'd had a hard time settling down since Aaron's call hours ago. Finally he'd decided steak and a beer would calm the twitchy feeling.

For two years he'd been the alpha of Mountain Pack, which technically covered about a four-hundred-mile territory, though ninety percent of the pack lived within a twenty-mile radius. His Uncle Samuel had been alpha before that, but he'd retired and Zach had moved up to take the position. Since then, there'd been no major problems. Hearing that a rogue wolf was living unannounced within his territory definitely constituted a problem. The question was how major it would be.

"Hey, it's Aaron. I'm about two and a half hours from your place and I need to see you." The tension in his brother's voice was loud and clear. Zach put the beer he'd been pulling out of the fridge back and grabbed a soda instead. Shit.

"You all right?"

"Yeah," Aaron sighed. "Just tired."

Zach concentrated on the bond he had with all his wolves and felt the exhaustion pulling at his brother. He closed his eyes and sent a burst of energy through their link.

"Thanks, Alpha." Aaron sounded grateful.

"You're welcome. You changed?" Zach caught himself, shook his head. "No, don't answer that. You would have told me if there was anything we needed to deal with before you got here. I'll wait. You need anyone else here?"

"No, just you for now. I don't think it will take long to explain, and you'll probably need some time to think things over. We don't actually need to do anything before tomorrow."

"All right, I'll be here."

Returning to his steak, he ate mechanically, his thoughts running rampant. It worried him that Aaron had made the change. It would have taken something fairly extreme to prompt such a thing, knowing how exhausted it would leave him before his long drive. Wolves rarely changed for only a few hours and usually expected to rest afterward.

Other than being tired, his brother was obviously all right. Zach would have known if he'd been hurt. Besides, Aaron was a powerful wolf. He was a couple of years older than Zach, and while he'd always been the more laid-back brother, he was fourth in the hierarchy. Whatever situation he'd encountered, he should have been able to handle it.

Reminding himself that his brother wasn't hurt only helped a little as he finished his meal. Distracting himself with other business, so that he would be able to devote his attention to whatever problem Aaron was bringing him, helped some more. Finally his security system alerted him that a vehicle was approaching. He watched from the window as his brother pulled up and turned off the ignition but didn't get out. The tension he'd managed to slough off reemerged full force. He opened the door.

Aaron looked right at him for a second before getting out of the truck. He made his way slowly up the walk as if waiting for something to happen. And then it did. The scent of a wolf not his brother or his brother's mate carried to him on the breeze. Not his pack, either. Something more, something special, something *his*. His blood sang, his breathing picked up, and when Aaron stopped some feet away, his wolf protested, wanting to get a better grasp of his mate's scent.

He grabbed the doorframe to keep from charging his brother. "Where is she?" he managed to get out without growling.

Aaron's gaze fixed on Zachary's shoulder. "About three hours away, little town called Slade. There's a problem." His eyes flicked to Zach's when his brother growled and he hurried on.

"She's okay, she's fine." He walked slowly closer.

"Why is her smell all over you?" Zach heard the tension in his own voice, but couldn't stop it.

Aaron dropped to his knees, lowering his head a little more, and didn't say anything.

Zach breathed deeply, pushing his power down. "Go take a shower." He stepped back into the house and headed to the living room. "Please."

As his brother hurried to wash the scents from his body, Zach paced his living room. He repeated the other man's words to himself, over and over. "She's okay, she's fine."

Aaron was back quickly, wearing a clean pair of jeans and t-shirt and smelling strongly of the soap from the guest bathroom. Zach tried out a smile, though he didn't think it was very genuine.

"Did you use the whole bottle?"

His brother sat at the far end of the sofa. "Almost."

"Tell me."

"She's beautiful and strong. She's young, twenty-four, but not so young. She has her own shop and loyal friends. She has no pack." Aaron took a breath but continued before Zach could ask the obvious question.

"She was attacked four years ago, raped and turned. She escaped when they didn't think she would live and has never spoken to a werewolf since. She knows nothing about us and was obviously hoping to keep it that way." The silence following that statement was huge.

With enormous effort, Zach maintained control, though he didn't particularly want to. He wanted to strike out, strike back, hurt those who had hurt his mate. But he needed to hear the rest, needed to find out who had hurt her, so he reined it in.

"Did you fight?" he asked, when he thought he could control his voice. Aaron's face was gratifyingly shocked. "What? No! No, of course not."

"If she didn't understand, if she attacked you—"

"No." Aaron took a deep breath, hanging his head. "When she told me, I didn't...I couldn't...I'm sorry, Zach, but I lost it. I had to change and go into the woods. Run it off, the need to kill something, to find them, hunt them and kill them. I couldn't pull it back and I had to change and leave her sitting there, after telling me what she did."

The pain radiating from his brother pulled at him. As his alpha, it was Zach's job to comfort and support his wolf. The need to fulfill that obligation helped him to find his control. He walked to the couch and sat heavily beside his brother, shoulders touching, and let out a deep sigh.

"I was just wishing I could do the same. Tell me the rest, Aaron. Please?"

Aaron turned to look at him, staring into the eyes of his brother, not his alpha, showing him all the empathy, all the rage that he had felt, that he still felt. Zach nodded his understanding.

Clearing his throat, Aaron told him. "I don't think she's ever told anyone about it, not even as if it was just a rape. She didn't go into details, she just...I think it already had taken a huge amount of control to not attack me on sight, to get me out of her shop, away from her friend, away from her town, and then stand there and wait to see what I would do." Aaron let his head drop back to the couch. "Damn, Zach, I don't even know if she was aware that she could beat me. I think she was ready to give it her all, kill me or die trying, if that's why I was there."

"She's strong?" Pride colored Zach's voice.

"Hell, she had me baring my belly within five minutes," Aaron grumbled, though he smiled. He straightened back up. "Listen, Zach, I know neither of us is exactly Mr. Sensitive but you're going to have to be really careful not to push her too fast. She doesn't know anything about werewolves, let alone about mates. I told her I would call her tomorrow." He paused, looking Zach over, judging his reaction. "Why don't you get some rest and I'll come back early in the morning with Tracy and we can talk about what might be the best way to do this, before we call her."

Zach grunted and heaved himself off the couch. "Be here early," he said as he walked out of the room.

HILLARY WOKE UP FEELING...STRANGELY calm. It seemed to her she should be more upset, but really she just sort of felt relieved. She'd been confronted with her nightmare, and it hadn't been bad at all. Of course, she really had no way of knowing for sure how much Aaron Jenner had been acting like himself, or if he'd been acting that way to get her to drop her guard. Although, if that had been his plan he had certainly succeeded yesterday afternoon and not taken advantage. But it was always possible he had a more long-term goal in mind than just attacking her in the woods, alone. Maybe he was waiting, gaining her trust while he gathered the other men.

The truth of the matter was, however, that her wolf instincts told her he'd been completely honest in word and action. She just didn't know to what degree she could trust these instincts. Yes, she had some experience with being able to smell lies and deception on a person, as well as honesty and compassion, but surely people who knew about such things could learn to mask them? She had no idea, but apparently it was time she learned.

Regardless, none of that really told her what this "pack" that he spoke of might be like. She thought that she could smell something on him, something separate from his own true scent, that meant pack. She would have to meet another werewolf to be sure, however, and right now she wasn't entirely sure she wanted to do that. Of course, the way Aaron had spoken of the laws, it might not really be her choice. It bugged her to realize that there were apparently laws and rules that she was meant to be abiding by and she had no idea what they were, let alone if she would be willing to follow them.

Hungry, she went to make breakfast. She'd called Stephen yesterday after parting with Aaron, telling him to take the rest of the day off. She would need to put in a good day's work to make up for what hadn't been done yesterday. She wanted to get the mayor's bed finished so he would have time to come look at it and make any changes before his wife's birthday next week.

She ate breakfast, showered and headed out to work. The office phone was ringing as she unlocked the door and she hurried to catch it before the voice mail picked up.

"Hello, Larry's Woodworking, may I help you?" She dropped her purse and keys on the desk.

"Ms. Abbott, this is Aaron. I was going to leave a message with my contact information, since I didn't think you would be in this early."

"Oh please, call me Hillary, or Larry or Hill, or whatever. Anything but miz," Hillary said, trying not to tense up at the sound of his voice. "I need to catch some things up from yesterday so I'm in a little bit earlier than normal." She sat down and got a pen and paper. "What's your information?"

Aaron gave her his numbers as well as his brother's. "Zachary is the alpha, I explained to him what I knew, and he wanted me to let you know that we, the whole pack, are here for you, but especially him. He's disgusted with the way an entire pack has obviously gone wrong in a big way and wants you to know that it will be taken care of, once we know more." Aaron took a breath, sounding nervous to Hillary, but also earnest.

"Larry, Zach is personally going to see to it that you have whatever you need as far as information, support, time, whatever. And I want you to know that I would be honored if you would consider me your friend and come to me for anything you might need as well. My wife wants to drive down there right now and meet you and take you to lunch and shopping or whatever, and tell you all about every unmated male wolf in our pack." He chuckled, clearly amused by his wife's girlie behavior.

"She's not worried about...I mean, she doesn't think that anything happened yesterday..." Hillary wasn't sure how to say it without sounding like an idiot.

Aaron gave a surprised bark. "No, no, of course not. You wouldn't know this, but mated...uh, married wolves don't have to worry about that—we mate for life. It would never occur to her to worry about something like that because it's just not an issue. Listen, I should have told you about this yesterday, but I didn't think of it. There's a website that gives a lot of detail about werewolves. The laws, the pack structure, information about the different packs, forums where people talk about whatever, the whole thing. It's totally password protected, secure, you have to have a login, all that fancy stuff, but obviously if someone managed to get in they would just think we were a bunch of crazy people, or playing a role-playing game or something. I thought you might like to check it out, get some information." He gave the details.

"I appreciate your not pushing me, Aaron, but it seems kind of like you're holding back on something and that's just making me more nervous," Hillary said bluntly. She liked this man, but she was going to be wary.

"Well, it's just that what I want to tell you won't really make sense until you know more facts. I think it will just upset you taken out of context. It's nothing bad, I swear. I was hoping you could check out the website and then maybe my wife Tracy and I could come meet with you, answer any questions you have, or do it over the phone, or you could come up here—whatever you're comfortable with."

"All right, I guess that sounds fair enough. I want you to know that clearly I can't really judge until I've met some more werewolves but I think I'm really glad that you're the guy I met first after all of these years. I'm not sure someone else could have handled it as well as you did, without pushing all of my buttons. I'm sure you're aware of how close to losing control I was yesterday, to shifting when I didn't want to." She waited, the silence growing longer.

Finally, Aaron answered. "I'm really glad to hear you say that, the first part. As for the second part, I think you underestimate yourself. I found your control to be pretty powerful. I'm not sure you understand how strong you are. I think you'll be surprised when you see what's on the website. When you read it, keep in mind that I'm fourth in a powerful pack. I have what is considered an above-average amount of power and control myself, and I was *not* able to keep from changing yesterday."

HILLARY MADE herself work hard through the day, staying away from the computer. She left work on time, picked up some dinner and went straight through the front door to her home office and booted up her computer. She input the information Aaron had given her and started reading.

What she found was fascinating and she barely remembered to eat her food. Apparently there were over two hundred packs in the country, with a national council, formed of first- and second-ranked wolves from the larger packs, to make and enforce the national laws. It was led by a president, who was elected by all the alphas across the country, whose job was to support, not rule, the council. She learned about the rankings, alpha then first through fourth, called the hierarchy, and discovered that there were about ten thousand wolves in the US, with around one thousand in the hierarchies.

She found that all wolves must show submission to the hierarchy, and that those in the hierarchy must show submission to those ranked above them. However, according to what she was reading, it wasn't a matter of choosing so much as a natural compulsion. Just as there was a compulsion to turn furry at the full moon, there was no need to ask another wolf if they ranked above you, you would just know. She didn't really get that, she hadn't felt anything weird when talking to Aaron, but the idea of feeling compelled to submit to a stranger was distinctly unnerving.

Well, that wasn't exactly true. She had felt comforted by his wolf, when he approached her in submission. She thought about what he'd said that morning, about being ranked fourth. He'd been preparing her for the fact that she was more powerful than he was.

She went back to the website, looking further into the ranking system. She was surprised again. According to the information, it was fairly rare for changes in the hierarchy to occur through violence. Most of the time it just worked out that when an alpha was ready to retire, step down into a position of advice rather than leadership, there was almost always someone already in line, growing more powerful and ready to take on the alpha position.

She found that hard to believe and hit the forums to see what the werewolves had to say about it. There were some stories about terrible instances of families and packs being torn apart by fighting, but she got the sense that these were just tales, entirely made up or grossly exaggerated. More like urban legends. The follow-up comments seemed to agree, and there never seemed to be hard facts of dates and locations.

Still, if what she was reading was true, then what Aaron was hinting at was that she was powerful enough to be a member of the hierarchy. She decided she was jumping ahead of herself. She had no idea if she wanted to have anything to do with these people. She didn't need them. She would meet with Aaron and his wife, ask questions, see how comfortable she felt. It was likely that she wouldn't want to have anything to do with them, and wouldn't have much contact after promising to follow the laws if they left her alone in her little town.

She was perfectly happy here with her shop and her best friend Todd and his wife, with Stephen and her other friends and neighbors. What did she need with a pack? There were bound to be far more disadvantages than advantages to getting involved with these wolves. Looking at the clock, Hillary realized she'd been at the computer for hours.

She typed a quick email to Aaron, letting him know that she had started looking at the information available on the website and would look some more. She knew he wanted to talk to her in person and respected the fact that he hadn't pushed for more. He certainly deserved it after letting her cry into his fur for so long the previous day. She decided to make the first offering, rather than leave him to worry about how soon he should ask for it himself. She asked if he and his wife would like to meet for lunch over the weekend.

She sent the email then checked through her own. Aaron was obviously sitting at his own computer, because he replied before she had finished going through her inbox. He and Tracy would love to meet her for a late lunch tomorrow or Friday, but if that wasn't possible, lunch on Saturday would be great, and would she mind terribly if Zachary joined them?

Hillary had to laugh. Part of her wanted to put it off until the weekend, but she figured she would just spend that time compulsively searching the website for more information and freaking herself out. She was not at all sure that she was ready to meet an alpha, but she figured a public restaurant was as good a place as any to feel him out, so she replied her acceptance for the next afternoon. If she was going to do this, she might as well do it now.

CHAPTER FOUR

Hillary skipped lunch and left work early. She arrived at the restaurant first and asked for an outside table. Choosing a seat facing the parking lot, she ordered an iced tea. She wasn't at all sure she would be able to go through with this. She felt, in the pit of her stomach, that her life was about to change forever. She tried to shake the feeling off, told herself that she was being fanciful, or pessimistic, or just plain nervous, but she didn't really believe it.

She saw Aaron Jenner get out of the backseat of a black SUV, going to the front passenger door to help a woman out. She took in the man getting out of the driver's side, seeing the resemblance to his brother. Tall and well built, he was attractive and she could sense the power in him from where she sat. They'd seen her as well, Aaron raising his hand to acknowledge her, his brother giving her a brief nod. They went into the restaurant and Hillary stood, waiting for them to come out to the patio. Aaron led his wife toward Hillary, his brother—no, Hillary reminded herself, his alpha— following behind.

"Hillary, I'd like to introduce you to my wife, my mate, Tracy. Tracy, this is Hillary Abbott, otherwise known as Larry." Aaron's smile was warm and genuine as he introduced the two women. He kept one hand on his wife at all times, making Hillary recall the article she'd read last night on the website, how wolves found comfort in touch. It wasn't just a sexual action, or a family action. All pack members touched each other in comfort or support or just friendship. The idea had made her nervous. Tracy stepped back to her husband's other side, leaving the way clear for the large man behind her. He put his hand out and Hillary took it. Her heart rate sped up and her breathing quickened. Her eyes were on his and neither looked away. She realized that he was also breathing harshly. She barely heard Aaron make the introduction.

"Hillary, this is Zachary, our pack alpha, my younger brother. Zach, this is Hillary." The top of Hillary's head came up to Zach's chin, so she was tilted up slightly to keep eye contact as he drew in closer. He kept her hand in his, bringing it up to his lips. He brushed a kiss across her knuckles. Hillary found the gesture, which should have been absurd, so sweet that it jolted her out of the trance she felt as if she had fallen into.

She stepped back, jerked her hand from his and sat down in her chair, not caring if that left the others hovering above her. She picked up her iced tea and took a drink, trying to get her breathing under control.

Aaron held a chair out for his wife and sat next to her, leaving the chair next to Hillary for Zach. Hillary ignored him and looked straight ahead at Tracy, offering her a slight smile. She realized then that she hadn't yet said a word. She had no idea what to say, however, and just wasn't capable of coming up with small talk, so she said nothing.

Tracy and Aaron both looked at Zach. Hillary picked up her menu and studied the lunch items. When Zachary spoke, she felt a betraying shiver go through her body.

"Mountain Pack welcomes you to our territory. If there is anything we can do to aid you, please just ask. We have a couple hundred acres of land that are available to all our wolves whenever they like, and we always gather for the full moon to run together. You're welcome to make use of them as well. I just ask that you call me first. If there are going to be other wolves out it will be necessary to introduce you, let them know they might run into a strange wolf."

As he spoke, Zach let his leg lean into Hillary's under the table. Although it was a natural act, she was pretty sure it had been deliberate. She considered shaking it off, but decided to concentrate on the conversation for now. His leg was deliciously warm against hers and somehow she drew strength from that warmth.

"I have plenty of forest near where I live for when I let myself change. I don't like to change at the full moon, but thank you for the offer." She looked up at Tracy who had gasped. "I'm sorry, was that rude? I appreciate the offer, it's just not necessary." She looked over at Aaron. He was smiling at her, so she relaxed again.

It was Zachary who answered her question. "Very few wolves are powerful enough to resist the change at the full moon. Some of the weaker wolves need help making the change, but if they don't they become sick and could eventually die. That's one of the reasons that we gather together as a pack. It's easier for them to make the change when they're surrounded by others using that power."

Hillary turned to Zach. Her eyebrows drew together as she processed this information. "I guess now that I think about it, I could feel the pull of power when Aaron changed near me. I was concentrating on holding back my power already, so I didn't really think about it at the time." She saw the way the men looked at each other, Aaron smiling with pride. She didn't want to think about what that was all about, so she went back to looking at her menu.

"How often do you change?" Aaron interrupted her reading.

She looked at the menu for another second, finalizing her choice, then folded it closed and looked at him. "Every other month or so. It depends on my schedule, what's going on in town that I need to be a part of. I usually skip the months that the tourists are at their most numerous, just in case they go deeper into the woods than usual. If I wait too long I tend to get overtired and cranky. It took me a while to figure out the balance."

Tracy leaned forward. "Balance in what? Why don't you just

change monthly and then you won't get sick?" She sounded fascinated, which made Hillary realize her habits were unusual. She squirmed a little bit, not really wanting to answer.

Tracy must have picked up on that because she sat back with an embarrassed look. "I'm so sorry, you don't have to answer that. I don't mean to pry." She seemed ready to launch into a full apology, so Hillary stopped her.

"Don't worry about it. I'm curious about how you guys do things. No reason for you not to be curious too. I guess it's just not something I give a lot of thought to. I think it mostly comes down to being stubborn. When I was attack—" She swallowed hard and could swear she felt Zach's leg pressing just a little bit more firmly into hers. "When it happened, they left me on the ground under the full moon. I didn't know what was going on, but I could feel this...this..." She broke off, looking away.

Aaron put his hand over hers on the table and Zach leaned in closer so that his arm met hers.

"I guess now I know that I was feeling the power building up, but I didn't know what it was and even though it sort of felt good and was taking away some of the pain, it freaked me out, and I held it off for as long as I could. For hours. Long enough I guess that they thought I wasn't going to change, so they left me to bleed to death as a human, went off running as wolves, came back, and everybody left." She took a drink of her iced tea.

"I waited until all the lights in the house went off before I gave in to that feeling. So, when it happened again at the next full moon, I got pissed off and I stayed awake the whole night fighting it off." She shrugged, looking back at Tracy, seeing sorrow and sympathy as well as surprise on her face. The waiter came up then and Hillary gave him her order while the others hastily checked their menus. Aaron gave her hand a little squeeze then let go.

When the waiter had left, Zachary picked up the conversation. "We'd like to hear all about you, both your past and your present, but it's important to all of us that you be comfortable with us. If you would rather ask us some questions first, I'm sure there's a lot you'd

like to know. But if you'd rather put off any werewolf talk until you're ready, we understand. Tracy could talk to you for hours just about her son, Ryder." He said this last bit with a perfectly straight face, but winked at his brother.

He hadn't moved his arm away from Hillary's, nor his leg. She found herself leaning in to him slightly, breathing deeply. She loved the sound of his voice. It was low and a little bit rumbly. She wanted to hear him say her name. Her pussy gave a little clench at the thought and she jerked away from him and up out of her seat. Her eyes were wide as she stared down at the three people.

They had all tensed at her movements, but remained seated, trying not to startle her further. Tracy and Aaron both had their gazes locked firmly below her face. With another man she would have been irritated, thinking he was looking at her breasts instead of her face, but with Aaron she was satisfied that he was lowering his gaze from hers. She looked at Zach. He looked her in the eyes, and his were smoldering.

She wasn't sure if she should be glad that he seemed to be feeling the same ridiculous desires she was, or terrified. She was edging toward terrified, and she took another step back. Zachary raised his hands slightly off the table, a gesture she recognized as showing her he was harmless. She gasped out a laugh, incredulous to realize that on the one hand she was freaking out over her body's instinctual responses that defied logic, but on the other hand she was reassured just the same over a similar response, because logic told her that there was no way this man was harmless.

And yet her wolf understood what the action meant—he was not bowing down to her strength, but he was promising not to attack or overpower her. She was trusting the very instincts she was fighting so hard to deny. All at once she was exhausted, the stress of the previous day, the crying jag, the effort it had taken to push down her power and resist the change, and the emotions. God, the emotions!

For years she'd tried to force this part of her life, this wolf she tried to abhor despite not always succeeding, to the very minimum she was capable of keeping it to. Now she couldn't escape it, couldn't even sit down with these people without feeling things she shouldn't be feeling. It was just not possible for a human being to have these kinds of reactions to a man just because he was sitting next to her, just because he had a sexy voice, or his leg was warm behind his jeans.

She recognized the fact that she was just freaking herself out more, the more she thought about how ridiculous this whole situation was. The more she freaked out, the harder it was to control, and that just freaked her out even more! She hadn't made the change in six weeks, and it pissed her off that she was feeling so close now, so weak and tired. As she had *that* night, so weak from the attack and the rapes and the pain and the blood loss. She wanted to sit down and cry again, as she had yesterday, just put her arms around Zach and sob, which was crazy. She hadn't cried for four years until yesterday and now she was just a mess.

The other diners on the patio were starting to look at her. The waiter came up to drop drinks off for the others and gave her a questioning look. Tracy thanked him and he left.

"Hillary, please let us help. This must be the most overwhelming thing that's happened to you since you were attacked and we don't want that. We can help make it easier, if you'll let us." Zach kept his voice low and calm, yet she could hear the concern in his voice.

If she had heard anything else, frustration or anger or even pity she would have turned and left. None of that was there. His eyes were compassionate and still held enough lust in them to make her ache. She closed her eyes and took a deep breath. Opening them, she glanced around at the other tables. "I don't want to be here," was all she could get out.

She took another step back. Zach rose, very slowly, watching her reactions. "Then we'll go. We can go into the woods, or to your house, to my house or Aaron's. There's a park not too far from here. Or we can sit in the car." He stepped away from his chair, putting his napkin on the table. "Just please don't ask us to go away."

There was a slight hint of fear in that last part and somehow that made it easier for Hillary. She gave a very small nod and turned and walked into the restaurant and out to the parking lot. She knew Zach was following her, could smell him coming closer as she stopped at the sidewalk. He came up behind her, his actions slightly hesitant, and put his hands on her shoulders very lightly. She breathed deep and leaned back just the tiniest bit. His arms came forward and he wrapped them around her shoulders, stepping into her so that she was leaning back against him. He rested his cheek on her head.

"Ah God," he muttered, squeezing her a bit more tightly. "Don't think for one second that this isn't scaring the shit out of me too," he whispered in her ear. "They're paying for the drinks. Where would you like to go?"

"I want to run," she whispered.

He tensed and she continued quickly, "Not away, just run. In the woods, as a wolf. I've never...*wanted*...to do that before. It's weird." She swallowed.

"It's natural," he disagreed. "And would make all of us feel better, I think. Things are simpler when we're wolves. Your brain forgets to worry over everything so much, to analyze everything. It's more...free."

"I'm not sure that I'll be able to, but I want to be outside, in the woods. I think it will make it easier to talk, at the very least."

"Will you drive with us, or let one of us drive with you? Please?" She thought from the way he sounded that he wasn't used to having to ask for things he wanted that badly very often.

"I wanted to ask Tracy a couple of questions." She could tell he was disappointed but he didn't argue. Aaron and Tracy came out of the restaurant then, and he let her go.

"Will you follow us?" he asked her.

"Okay." Hillary headed to her car without looking back. Tracy came up beside her but remained silent as they got inside. They drove for a couple of minutes before Hillary broke the silence.

"So this, uh, mate thing. How's that really work?" She swallowed hard and stared straight ahead, not ready to meet Tracy's gaze.

Tracy settled herself back into the seat and Hillary didn't have to see her smile to know it was there.

"It can be pretty powerful. One of the interesting things about it is that the more powerful the couple, the stronger the attraction. For example, my sister, who is not and will never be, in the hierarchy, dated her mate for a month before they had sex and found out for sure that they were mates. She suspected, but she wasn't desperate to fuck him and know for sure. When I first met Aaron, we barely managed to separate after the first date without sex, and only made it through half a movie on the second date before leaving and going to the nearest motel. We were so hot for each other, there really wasn't a question as to being mates. He was just trying to give me some time because I was so nervous."

"If you knew he was your mate, why were you nervous? Were you afraid you wouldn't get along with him?"

Tracy laughed gently. "No, I was afraid I wasn't good enough for him, that I wasn't experienced enough for him, powerful or beautiful or talented enough for him."

Hillary glanced at her passenger in time to see Tracy blush and duck her head.

"I'm from a smaller, less powerful pack and I'd heard about how strong Mountain Pack was. It's hard to understand until you've completed the mating, but it really is magical. I mean, I was so nervous, but also *so hot* for him. It's not like he's perfect, of course, and I certainly am not to him. You still have to be willing to compromise, to be kind to each other, not take each other for granted, but...there's just more. When you mate, you can actually feel your souls connect. It's hard to be apart from him for more than a few hours, let alone days. When he comes home, we have to touch, just a bit, just for a minute, to reconnect. When your mate is upset or unhappy, you feel it and it hurts you. So it's not like human relationships, where one person can hide their unhappiness, or just not care that their partner isn't happy and fulfilled."

Hillary squirmed in her seat. Just hearing about it somehow

made the ache she was still feeling slightly stronger. And yet it was nothing compared to what she'd felt when Zach touched her.

"I was telling you about how strong it is for powerful wolves. I was mated with Aaron before his sister Molly mated with her husband Travis. Molly is first in our pack, and Travis was first with New England. They met at Travis' cousin's wedding to one of our wolves. Aaron and Molly and I flew out there to support Heidi, our pack mate, for her wedding, and the moment Molly and Travis met, it was like the temperature in the house went up ten degrees, and everyone got horny vicariously." She smiled at the memory then shot Hillary a look. "Sort of like just now, at the restaurant."

Wincing at the idea that the couple had been aware of what she and Zach had been feeling, she decided to pretend ignorance and remained silent until Tracy continued with her story.

"They're both pretty powerful and very independent, so there was a lot of back and forth as they fought the idea of mating. Neither thought they were ready, and for some reason both had the misguided and ridiculous idea that their mate would be easygoing and biddable. Ha! As if someone that strong-minded would be happy with a mate who was willing to take a backseat. I think they made it to dessert before they had to find a room. We didn't see them at all the next day and when we finally did see them it was truly amazing to see how happy they were. Not that they don't still argue and constantly test each other, but you can see that they enjoy it, and each other."

Hillary thought about this as she followed the SUV into a campground. Zachary paid the attendant who waved Hillary through. They drove for another few minutes, to a lot near the back border of the campground. She parked next to the SUV, but made no move to turn off the car or unlatch her seat belt. She tightened both hands on the wheel, and looked at Tracy.

"There is so much feeling building up inside me right now and I know that some of it is him, but I don't think that's all of it. I'm afraid to let it loose, afraid of what else might come tearing out of me. It's not like I can separate it, can let some out and push the rest down, it's going to be all or nothing. I was only around him for half an hour and already so much is boiling inside me. I don't know if I can handle it boiling over right now." She rested her forehead on the steering wheel, between her hands.

Tracy reached over and laid a hand on her leg.

"You need to tell him that. I know Zach. Separate from the whole mate thing, I can tell you he's a good man. If there's one thing that I can promise you, it's that he won't run from you. There's nothing you can do or say that will make him back away from you. He'll do everything in his power to make whatever is troubling you better. And his power is considerable. I told you the more powerful the wolf, the stronger the mating hits you. You don't know him, so you probably couldn't see it, but Zachary was working very hard at that restaurant to be calm and controlled so that he wouldn't scare you."

Hillary rolled her head a bit so she could see the men as they stood next to the SUV, talking quietly, obviously waiting for the women to make their move.

"That doesn't mean he wasn't feeling everything you're feeling, just that he's strong enough to keep it from erupting, at least for a while. He knows that you're feeling everything that he is, but that you have it so much worse because you don't know about it and because you understandably relate everything about your wolf to the attack."

"I don't know that I want to be around someone who's as strong as you say he's being," Hillary confessed.

Tracy nodded. "I can completely understand that part of you feels that way. The part that was hurt by others stronger than you were. But you're alpha. You couldn't possibly stand for less. Hillary, believe me when I tell you that Zach has spent many hours since he first scented you on Aaron, since he first heard what you'd gone through, trying to figure out the best way to help you through all of this. That's his number one priority. He knows that you won't have the basic acceptance of this that he does, just because he's been

expecting this to occur all his life." Tracy opened her seat belt but made no move toward the door.

"Then, when he finally saw you, I have no doubt that his protective nature went into extreme overdrive. Really, it's amazing to me how strong he's been, to be separated from you in the cars, to not be opening your door right now to make sure you're all right."

A shiver went through her and Hillary popped her seat belt and started to get out of the car. Pausing, she reached her hand back to Tracy's, giving it a squeeze. "Thanks."

They got out of the car, rounding the front of it to meet up with the brothers. Zachary reached his hand out and Hillary took it, unable to resist the need to touch him or the need she felt from him to do the same.

"Can I talk to you for a few minutes?" he asked her.

She wanted to smile, say something to make this all easier somehow, but she couldn't, so she just gave him a small nod.

SHE HAD NO IDEA, Zach thought, that her eyes were huge in her face, or that the vulnerability she was showing when he was positive she was normally very strong and sure of herself, were enough to convince him completely that he was in love. He'd been sure before meeting her that she was his mate, and once they met, he was sure he wanted to fuck her for the next sixty or seventy years, but now...he just wanted to wrap her up in his arms, take away all of her doubts and fears.

When he'd first seen her sitting at the restaurant waiting for them, trying not to look nervous, he'd reminded himself that he had to be careful, go slowly. He'd worked hard not to stare, but she was so damn beautiful. Her blonde hair was long enough that the French braid reached past her shoulders. Her blue eyes, while wary, had sparkled with a power that called to his soul. It had been a struggle to sit down next to her, casually, rather than pick her up and cart her back to his SUV Though his desire to make her feel safe would have kept that from happening, there was also the small fact that she probably would have gutted him before he'd cleared the restaurant that really gave him pause. And had him hiding a smile.

"I think that you should change," he started, leading her toward a rough wooden bench. "Run around as a wolf with a pack for a bit, get to know us that way, without the complication of human worries and fears. It's easier to let those go, as I'm sure you've discovered, when your brain is otherwise occupied with more primal instincts."

She stiffened, took a deep breath and pulled her hand from his. "I—"

She gave an undignified squeak as he lifted her onto his lap, his arms holding her tightly to him.

She narrowed her eyes at him, demanding an explanation without saying a word.

"Do you think that I can feel your fear without doing something to make us both feel better?" He shrugged. "I'm sorry, really, but it's just not possible."

The stiffness went out of her abruptly and she dropped her head to his shoulder. "I thought changing into a wolf was surreal, but this day has topped that in the unbelievable category." She closed her eyes, turning her nose into his neck and breathing in his scent.

"I know that this is scary and I swear that if I thought it would help for me to back off, I would." He paused. "Well, I would try real hard, at least."

She snorted, then slapped a hand over her mouth.

"Ah hell, don't do things like that. It's hard enough for me not to throw you on the ground right now and..." he trailed off. "Shit, I'm sorry," he began, but she stopped him.

"No, it's okay. I understand what you meant. Well, I don't exactly understand how my snorting like a pig makes you feel that way, but the rest..." She smiled into his neck.

"Believe me," he said, after a moment. "It's as much a surprise to me as it is to you." They both laughed.

"Why does the idea of changing scare you? You've been doing it for four years, right?"

"What you said, about letting go of our human worries and thoughts, that's what scares me. It always has, since the moment I realized that I was going to become like *them*."

She shuddered and he resisted the urge to tighten his arms around her further.

"I guess, at the time, I tried to blame the fact that this whole group of people were evil *because* they were wolves, which meant that if I was a wolf too, I must have that evil inside me. Maybe if it had just been one or two, but twenty-some people? All perfectly willing to watch me be raped and mauled as the conclusion of their barbecue? It was just so damn *crazy*."

"It's natural that you would associate that evil with werewolves in general, especially having nothing else to compare with. But surely you realized after some time that there is nothing evil about you, whether in wolf or human form." He rested his cheek on the top of her head, tucking her more firmly against his shoulder.

"Since the very beginning I have been fighting this power inside, fighting to keep it contained as much as possible, to control it as much as possible. That's why I refused to change with the moon, or as often as my wolf obviously wanted to. I've never let it all loose, that feeling, that power, and I'm afraid if I do, that I'll lose myself, my humanity. That I'll become like them. Maybe not all at once, but gradually."

She pulled back so she could meet his eyes. Hers were filled with worry and concern and his heart squeezed tight in his chest as he realized that she was worried *for him*. Worried that her words would hurt him.

"Since I met you, that feeling is getting more and more restless, harder to contain. It's getting harder and harder to separate the...lust...from the rest of it. I'm afraid that if I give in to that, or if I change now while I don't have it all locked away and under control, that I'll...I don't know, go crazy I guess, or," she paused again, dropped her gaze from his, "evil."

Zach wrapped his calmness around her just as he had his arms around her. Her admission didn't worry him for a second. He wanted, needed, to find the right words to ease her fears.

Slowly she relaxed back against him.

"I understand how you came to those conclusions. I want to tell you that they're totally wrong and just expect you to forget about them, but obviously that's not possible. I can tell you that I've met very few really bad werewolves. I don't know why. I mean, if you look at the number of crazy humans, why shouldn't there be an equal percentage of crazy wolves? It would be logical, but it's just not the case. There are plenty of werewolves I don't particularly like, that I'm not anxious to hang out with, but I've only met a handful I would hesitate to allow into my pack." He paused, angling his head to breathe in the scent of her.

"We can deal with the evil that you've encountered later, when you're not feeling so conflicted. Right now I can tell you with absolute certainty that there is not a molecule of evil inside you. The goodness practically pours from you and the life you've led since that awful day is proof that even when evil did its very best to make you the same as them, it failed miserably. I am so proud." He had to swallow hard to keep talking. "*So* proud that you are mine, and that if I can prove myself to be half the person you are, you might consent to take me as yours."

She started to cry and his heart clenched. He was pretty sure it was a good cry, a cleansing cry, but it was still hard to watch. The fact that she held on to him tightly made it easier to believe that it was a good thing. Maybe he had found the right words.

After a little while, she pushed herself off his shoulder, giving a watery laugh. "Crying like a baby two days in a row. Maybe I'll just stay in bed all day tomorrow."

Zach grinned and wiped at her tears with his clumsy fingers. "I think that's an excellent idea. I'll make sure you don't get bored."

Who knew a blush could be so cute? The fact that she smiled helped him relax the tension that was still holding him hostage. He had to be so careful not to screw this up.

"Zach, I don't...I'm not..." She let the smile drop and looked him in the eyes, then just shrugged.

"Baby, you're going to have to take my word for it when I say that there is no way that our coming together could be anything less than extraordinary."

He laughed when she blushed again and caught her chin when she tried to duck her head. He leaned in, brushing his mouth against hers softly.

"I promise," Zach whispered, "that I will go as slowly as you need, even if it kills me." He paused then added with a huge grin, "Even if my balls turn blue and fall right off."

She laughed and smacked his shoulder.

"I'm not that naïve, you pathetic man." She sniffed, and turned toward Aaron and Tracy as the couple walked toward them.

"Pathetic," he agreed. "That's exactly what I'm prepared to be, just for you." He gave her puppy dog eyes and was gratified to see real warmth in her answering smile.

"I guess if there's a good time to do this, now would be it, out here with three powerful wolves to keep an eye on me."

Zach swallowed hard. He'd hoped he could do this, but after holding her so close, hearing her vulnerabilities prove how strong she really was, he had to admit that in this, he wasn't strong enough. He put his hand under her chin, meeting her eyes. "Two powerful wolves and one strong alpha," he said with regret, "who will be close if there's a problem. I wish that I could do this with you this time but there is absolutely no way that I could change right now and not have you. I consider myself a strong man and a strong wolf, but it's taking all of my control to give you the time you need. I just don't think I can do that while letting my wolf run free with you."

He didn't miss the flash of shame that crossed her face or the way her eyes dropped. She should be angry at him, not disappointed in herself. He growled, his fingers tightening on her chin when she tried to jerk back. "I didn't tell you that to upset you, or make you feel guilty or ashamed. I told you that because it's the truth and I won't give you anything less than the truth. I will always trust you with the truth of what I'm feeling and I ask you to do the same."

Her eyes lowered and her shoulders relaxed. "I'm getting tired of feeling weak in front of you."

He barked out a surprised laugh. "Damn, Larry, do you really have no idea of the power and strength you give off? Nobody here thinks you're weak. I can't imagine even the clueless humans think you're weak. I know only the tiniest bit of your story and already I'm amazed at how strong and capable you are. You should be angry at me for not having the strength to do this with you and still give you the time and space you need. I can only thank the incredibly strong mating attraction for keeping you from leaving me behind before you have a chance to get to know me, to find that I'll be strong enough to love and support you. To deserve you."

He gave her a quick kiss on the lips, backing up from her before she had a chance to react.

"Now, go change, I'll start walking north. Just do me a favor and stay with Aaron and Tracy, please." He turned and started walking deeper into the woods.

HILLARY TOOK a deep breath and looked at the other two. "How do you guys do this? I usually pick a tree away from the campsite where I can leave my clothes."

Tracy answered. "When the whole pack is together, we all just get naked and change, pretty much at the same time, in the same place. In smaller groups, it usually feels a bit more intimate, so we basically do like you said. People find their own spot, change, and meet up back in the middle." She grabbed Aaron's hand and pulled him off to the right.

Hillary moved a bit to the left, found a good spot and quickly took off her shoes and clothes. She gave herself one minute to be nervous then focused on the feeling inside, the power which had begun to change since meeting Zachary. It felt even stronger now,

but also more complete somehow. As if there had been pieces missing because of the way she'd been changed, and Zach had filled them in just by being there.

She felt her wolf, there was no need to call her forth, merely to stop holding her back, and suddenly the world was bigger. The information flooding her brain was disorienting for half a second, as it always was, her brain adjusting to the massive quantity of stimulus that her human senses didn't accumulate. Almost immediately her nose pinpointed one scent above all the others crowding around her and she gave a bark of joy and followed it to Zach.

The large brown and gold wolf she knew to be Aaron and a smaller, lighter brown wolf were coming toward her, but they stopped abruptly as she swept past, anxious to find Zach. He heard her coming and turned around, spotting her. He went to his knees and she slowed her run, walking up to him.

She was big enough that on his knees they were face-to-face. She gently nudged his jaw, which for some reason had dropped open, with her snout. His teeth clacked shut audibly and his hands inched their way into her fur. She gave his cheek a lick, liking the taste of him. She had never been close to a human when in wolf form and she let herself explore this man, her mate. She'd been mostly convinced that he was her mate, even in the restaurant, the feelings running through her too extreme to be mistaken, but now...now she had no doubt, no hesitation. She barked at him, wanting his wolf to come play with her.

"Christ, you're beautiful."

She loved the sound of his voice. His hands were running up and down her sides, clutching at then smoothing her fur. He brought them to her head, scratching behind her ears for a minute. Her eyes half closed at the heavenly sensation. She heard Aaron and Tracy behind her and wondered what had taken them so long.

Hillary turned enough that she could see the wolves behind her but kept her body pressed into Zach's. She stood, strong and proud in the circle of his arms and looked at her wolves. In this form there was no question but that she was a part of them and they were a part of her. This was pack, her pack, and these were her wolves.

She was amazed that she'd been so ignorant of this feeling while sharing time with them as a human. Would she feel this way with every wolf she met? Know without being told which wolves were her pack? Suddenly she couldn't wait to find out, to meet others of her kind.

Aaron approached her first, lowering his larger body so that his head was beneath hers. She wondered if Zach's fur had gold like this, highlighting the brown. He came to her as he had once before, dropping fully to the ground at her feet, baring his throat and belly. She leaned down, nuzzling his throat for a moment, giving it an affectionate lick. She liked that this man would be her friend regardless of her relationship with Zach.

She thought the same would be true for Tracy, hoped it would be. She looked toward the smaller wolf and Tracy came forward, also low to the ground and offered her throat and belly. Her fur was much lighter than Aaron's, fawn-colored, and Hillary thought they made an attractive pair. She gave Tracy a playful nudge in the side, a little nip, and bounced out of Zach's arms. The three wolves circled each other for a moment, then Hillary broke free and started to run.

They raced and played, always circling around so that they were never far from Zach as he continued to hike farther into the woods. The simple act of running with the two wolves gave Hillary such pleasure, as if she had come home. She raised her head and howled, pleased when they joined in with her. After a time she led Aaron and Tracy back to Zach who had found a good place to stop. She curled up next to him, giving him her warmth on one side while Aaron and Tracy warmed his back, and fell asleep with Zach's fingers stroking her gently.

The nightmare snuck up on Hillary, as it often did when she had run her wolf to exhaustion. Her wolf brain tended to shy past the memory of the initial attack and concentrate on the confused wolf who'd risen from the battered woman that early morning, exhausted and yet strangely exhilarated as power coursed through her.

She whimpered in the remembered fear of being found before she could get away, her feet twitching in sympathy to that long-ago wolf who had pushed herself on and on, despite her weariness and confusion. That initial transition had somehow healed the horrible neck wound left from Jeff's attack of her, as well as the sharp pain from the rapes.

To this day she had no idea how far she'd traveled that morning before she heard the baying far behind her. She'd been nearing her dropping point but that sound had served to push her on for hours more. By the time night came she could no longer hear any sounds of pursuit. She'd been relieved to pass out of the desert and into the mountains, searching out every stream she could smell, running in the shallow streambeds when she could manage it. Finally, when she could run no more, she found a spot that was dense with brush and fell asleep.

Remembering her fear of being found while sleeping, Hillary jerked awake only to feel the soothing caress of Zach's hands on her body. His head had been pillowed on her shoulder as he slept but now he was lifted up on his side, whispering calming words into her ear, letting her know that she wasn't alone, that she was safe. She turned, nudging him to his back, and lay with her chin and one paw on his stomach. Tracy rose sleepily from the other side of Aaron, and came around to curl up at Hillary's side and they all fell back to sleep.

In the morning they made their way back to the car. For the most part the wolves stayed with Zach, only occasionally darting off, always circling back within minutes to his side. When they got to where the clothes were, Zach followed Hillary to her tree.

He buried his face in her ruff, inhaling her scent. "I can't wait for the day when I can watch you change from beautiful woman to gorgeous wolf and back again. I have never seen such a wolf as you, pure white with your glowing blue eyes. I want to run through the woods with you, I want to mount you and make you mine in every way possible. But most of all, I want you to know, for sure, to the depths of your soul, that I am yours."

Hillary whined at him, licking his ear. He gave her one last stroke and stood. "Soon, please God, let it be soon," he said and walked to the cars.

CHAPTER FIVE

Hillary forced herself to work hard all day. The work that normally brought her such peace and contentment was fighting a losing battle today. She placed her inability to focus squarely on Zach's head. Like a damn teenager, she'd found herself wondering what it would feel like to sleep against his chest when she wasn't furry. Her hands itched to run through his nearly black hair, to tease him about the silver running through it. She wanted to know what his favorite color was and what he liked to read. She felt jittery and was sure that she was being a moody bitch. Which Stephen confirmed late in the day as he cleaned up.

"What's your deal today, Larry? You need to get laid?" He ducked the cleaning rag she hurled at him, chuckling. "Damn, I was just joking but I guess I was more right than I knew!" He picked the cloth up and put it in the bin. "Seriously, what's the deal? I can't imagine any guy you set your sights on being hard to catch."

Hillary stared at him, astonished. "What are you talking about? Nobody in this town has ever even asked me out."

Stephen snorted. "Only because you're wearing a huge 'Do Not Disturb' sign on your forehead at all times. Believe me, they're constantly checking to see if it's still there so they can work up the nerve to approach you without having to worry about getting their dicks sliced off." He laughed again, obviously amused by her expression.

"I didn't realize it was a subconscious thing. I thought it was deliberate or I would have told you how many times guys have approached me to find out what you were waiting for." He brushed her cheek with a kiss then opened the door. "Why don't you come over for dinner? You can tell me who's got you all worked up and I can moan and groan about the lack of gay men in this area. We can call Todd and Maria, see if they want to join us and we can all pick on Todd just for being a man."

"Thanks, Stephen," Hillary sighed, closing and locking the shop door. "But I know who I need to see to fix this problem. I've just been working my way around to it." She was sure she was blushing so she narrowed her eyes at him, daring him to comment.

"Larry, you know if you need to talk about anything, I'm here for you."

Well, shit. Now she felt like an idiot. She gave his cheek a quick kiss. "I know, Stee, thanks." She got in her car and drove the short distance to her house.

When she got inside, Hillary walked straight to the phone so that she wouldn't chicken out. She'd left Zach's number there so that she wouldn't be too tempted to call him from work. She'd needed the day, needed to try to soothe herself with work while she came to terms with the fact that she was incapable of refusing this whole mate thing.

Intellectually she felt that if she kept away from Zachary for long enough, this itchy feeling, this *need* to touch him, to be with him, would eventually go away, but truthfully she just didn't want to fight the wonderful feelings. Her wolf was urging her to go to him and so was her heart.

If she stopped to think about it for too long, now that she'd admitted it, she'd freak herself out about letting this werewolf nature rule her. But it was time to come to terms with her reality

and to deal with the fact that she couldn't write off all werewolves as the evil beings she had dealt with. She dialed the number.

"Larry?" he answered, instead of saying hello.

She laughed. "Caller ID?"

"Yes. I've been afraid to be more than one ring away from this damn cell phone all day. I was worried about you. I know it's difficult, having to deal with the separation anxiety while trying to come to terms with all of this. I wish I could make it better for you." He sounded genuinely distressed and Hillary relaxed, knowing that she could love this man despite the fact that he was a werewolf, despite the fact that he was a strong, controlling alpha. In this case, the wolf's nature would aid her because he would find it difficult to do anything but help and support her any way that she needed him. And she would do the same for him.

She didn't try to explain her thinking to him, merely said, "I want to see you. I need to see you, but...I don't think I'm ready for the whole pack, especially while I'm feeling so...torn. Like a part of me is missing and only you can put me all back together again."

His strangled moan was muffled. "Baby, I'll come to you, that's not a problem, but I need you to be real clear on what you want from me when you see me, so that I don't screw this up. Do you want me to bring Aaron and Tracy so you can ask us more questions? Get to know us better?"

"Hell no!" she blurted. "I can't wait any longer, Zach, I need *you*. I'll meet you back by that restaurant. There was a little B&B there, right? It's off-season, so they should have a room for the weekend, right? Will you stay with me?"

The breathing on the other end of the line was harsh. "Baby, I think it might be better not to be surrounded by humans. My cousin Peter has a cabin about fifteen miles east of there. It's not super fancy or anything, but it's fairly isolated. Because, Hillary, I just don't think I'm going to be able to stay very quiet when I'm with you, at least not the first dozen times or so."

Hillary's breathing had sped up at the torment in Zach's voice. She managed a whisper. "Okay, email me the directions. I'm going to pack. I'll leave in an hour." She hung up the phone before he could say anything else and went to shower.

———

LESS THAN TWO HOURS LATER, Hillary pulled up to the cabin. The directions had been very specific, and she recognized the SUV in front of it. The door opened as she parked, and Zachary stood there waiting.

He seemed very tense as Hillary approached. She knew that he was being cautious, not wanting to make assumptions, not wanting to rush her. She walked up to him and kept going until she was fully against him, her face going naturally to the curve of his neck, his cock pressing into her stomach. She wrapped her arms around him and held on tight. His hands tried to pull her even closer, one arm around her shoulders, one settling possessively in the small of her back.

She took a deep breath, determined to be as honest with him as he had been with her. "Zach, I want this so badly, but I don't know...I'm guess I'm afraid I'll freeze up or hurt you..."

He squeezed her tight before moving one hand up to cradle her cheek. "Baby, the worst that could happen is that I have to run out and jump in the cold spring. Not a big deal. I'm not going to lie and say I'm not dying for you, but I'm already a hundred times better than I was an hour ago. As long as we're together, and as long as we talk to each other, we'll be fine, I swear." His fingers sifted through her hair and he pulled her head back gently so that he could kiss her.

Hillary sank into the kiss, pushing away any thoughts, letting the incredible feelings be everything. His lips were soft against hers, teasing her with their fullness. She waited for him to give her his tongue, but he played with her, using only his lips and the occasional nip. Finally she remembered that she was an alpha bitch, she didn't have to wait for him. She thrust her tongue into his mouth and was immediately rewarded by his groan of pleasure, by the tightening of his fingers in her hair and the grinding of his cock into her stomach. She smiled, interrupting the rhythm he had taken up, then pulled back.

His eyes were glassy and she knew a moment of deep satisfaction that this was her man, that she could do this to him just by being herself. She promised herself in that moment to try as hard as she could to remember who she was and what she had to offer, rather than remembering the victim she had been so long ago.

"Zach," she said, as he continued to stare at her unblinkingly.

"Huh?" he asked, reaching his hand out to brush her lower lip with his thumb.

She darted her tongue out to lick her lips and taste his thumb, then stepped back. He jerked forward, nearly grabbing her before he caught himself.

"What's wrong? Where are you going?" His eyes were a little bit wild now, no longer glassy.

She smiled gently at him, her breathing still coming hard and fast from just one kiss.

"I thought I would get my bag and that you might let me in," she said, picking the bag up from the porch where she'd dropped it while they spoke.

He blinked then grimaced. "I'm sorry, baby, let me take that." He took the bag and ushered her into the cabin.

It wasn't the rustic, bachelor's fishing cabin she'd expected, but a charming, open space, nicely furnished and clearly used often. There was the main room, with a fireplace and cozy sitting area on one side, and a small dining table on the other. She could see through the dining room into the kitchen that was nearly as large as hers. There were stairs leading up to the second floor where she figured the bedrooms were.

Zach grabbed her hand and headed up the stairs straight into a guest bedroom. As though he couldn't wait a moment longer, he pulled her back to him and resumed the kiss as if there'd been no break. Once there, however, he seemed in no hurry to push on. He kissed her as if he would be happy to do so for hours without stopping and she had no intention of stopping him. She pushed him back until he hit the bed with his legs. The bed was high and he turned her around and lifted her slightly so that she was sitting on the mattress. She opened her legs so that he could step between them.

Hillary explored his mouth and let him explore hers. They dueled in the middle for a time, before she broke off to nibble on his lower lip. He pulled her back in, thrusting in and out of her mouth in glorious abandon. Her hands alternated between fisting in his hair and running over his scalp, scratching gently then tickling his nape. He reciprocated, pushing his hands through her braid, undoing it to let her hair fall about her shoulders.

Hillary left one hand to play with his silky strands, the other following the line of his shoulder then curling around to explore his back. She became distracted by the feel of muscle and brought her other hand down to share in the newfound discovery. He left her to it for a time, before he followed suit.

The feel of his large, warm hands caressing her back was wonderful. Her hands itched to feel his bare skin and her back was begging to feel his hands directly. Without breaking the kiss, she pulled her torso back and raised his shirt up to his head. He did the same with hers, and they separated long enough to tangle arms and shirts until they were both free, then dove back together for more.

The first feel of his bare skin on her hands made Hillary gasp into Zach's mouth. She moaned when he ran his fingers up her spine then down her sides. She squeezed his shoulders, traced the lines of his muscles. Eventually her hands made it down to the small of his back and the waistband of his jeans.

On his next pass up her back Zach let his thumbs caress the sides of her breasts. Hillary was thankful she was sitting down, because she was pretty sure her knees wouldn't have supported her. She abandoned his back, pulled back from the kiss, and said, "Please." Zach must have known what she needed, because he brought his hands forward to unclasp her bra then slid the straps down her arms, tossing it to the bed behind her.

His beautiful gray eyes stared down at her, his expression radiating hunger and awe. Hillary felt no need to cover herself in the face of this devotion. She tracked her gaze down to his bare chest. She let her hands come up to feel the small amount of hair, traced his pecs then pushed her fingertips up, over his small nipples. She smiled in delight when he jerked.

Zach groaned as she found her new play area. She plucked and scraped at his nipples and finally he attacked her mouth again. She moved her hands up his arms and back to his hair, reveling again in the hungry kiss. He cupped her breasts, brushed his thumb over her nipples, smiling in retaliation when she jerked and moaned.

She broke the kiss again, looking down at his dark hands covering her pale breasts, and watched her chest swell even further with a deep gasp. He leaned down and drew one nipple into his mouth, lashing it with his tongue, biting it gently. "Oh shit, oh Zach, oh shit." She had no clue what she was muttering, only that it felt so good, too good. He switched sides, his fingers plucking at the now-wet nipple his mouth had abandoned, and Hillary cried out.

The seam of her jeans was thoroughly wet now and she tried to grind herself against it for some relief as he worked her breasts. Finally she couldn't stand it and yanked his head back up to her mouth. This time she let her hands explore farther down, finally realizing that he wasn't going to push into new territory with her tonight—that she would have to be the one to explore when and where she was ready, and he would follow.

He broke the kiss as her fingers dipped into his waistband, moving to unbutton and unzip him. "Larry, you taste so fucking good, you feel so fucking good." She kissed along his jaw then grabbed his earlobe. He shuddered as she sucked it into her mouth, his hands going back to her breasts. Every time she sucked, he squeezed, and her pussy clenched in support. She struggled to concentrate enough to get his pants started on the way down.

Zachary brought Hillary back off the bed, pulling his head out of her reach, his hands on hers as she started to push his jeans the rest of the way down. "Are you okay? Are you doing okay?" he managed to get out.

Hillary stared at him uncomprehendingly, her brow creased. "Not if you don't get those damn jeans off and maybe work on mine while you're at it," she answered finally.

He smiled. "Yes ma'am."

He must have realized she wasn't so sure about how to move things forward, because he finally took the lead. He shucked his jeans in two seconds flat, fell to his knees and began kissing her while working on her jeans. His mouth trailed over her breasts, kissing each nipple one more time, before moving down. His hands worked quickly, his mouth slowly, so that by the time his tongue reached her bellybutton, he had taken off her jeans and, she realized suddenly, her panties.

She'd never guessed her bellybutton could be the source of such pleasure! Her hands felt for the bed behind her, supporting her so she could remain standing. *His* hands, meanwhile, were learning the shape of her ass, then running down her thighs.

"Zach," she moaned raggedly. "Zach, I need..." She left off, not really sure how to finish, only wishing she could reach him better. She had to make do with fisting her hands in his short hair again. She tugged gently, then more sharply as he ignored her. She pushed his head back so his eyes were looking up to hers. "Please, Zach, I don't know what to do," she cried out, wanting so badly to make this right, to make him feel as good as she was feeling.

He lifted her up, laying her down on the bed. "Listen to me, Hillary, please listen, this is important," he managed, pulling himself together. He climbed up next to her, straddling her thighs, his hands on either side of her shoulders, his face looking intently into hers.

"If you touch me right now, I'm going to lose it. I need you to do this for me, this first time, or I won't be able to make it. It's just too good, you feel too damn good. I need you to let me do the touching. You hold on to the headboard, let me get you off a couple of times. I *need* to hear your pleasure before I get in you, because once I'm there, I don't think I'll be able to last."

She whimpered and frowned, her hands going to his chest. "Zach," she started.

"No, baby, please, I swear, next time you can touch me all you want, however long you want. Please, I'm begging you. Let me do it this way, this time."

He was so serious, so desperate, she had to give in. She looked him in the eye, showing him her trust, not only that he wouldn't hurt her, but that he'd make sure she felt nothing but pleasure.

Zach dropped a quick kiss on her in gratitude. "I swear, we'll have years to experiment and practice." He dropped down and kissed her chin then the hollow of her neck.

Hillary squirmed, certain she would kill him if he took the slow way down again, but he paused at her breasts for only a moment, jumped to her navel and picked up where he'd left off.

Leaving a wet trail, he made his way down, his hands gently leading the way. He cupped her first, pausing while she jumped then relaxed. His mouth nipped gently on her thigh as he held his hand steady. She squirmed underneath him, needing more. He kissed her other thigh, then used his thumbs to part her pussy. His breath was hot on her, and she had to hold the headboard tight to stay still.

"You are so beautiful. I don't know if I deserve you, but I do know I can't ever let you go."

She moaned, feeling his words on her, as much as hearing them. He nuzzled her with his nose then licked her gently. She bucked but he brought his hands underneath her butt and held her still. He kissed her pussy as he had her mouth, licking and sucking until she thought she would die.

The feelings building inside her were similar to the feeling of power, of wolf, of moon, but different. Out of her control and yet not frightening. He thrust his tongue into her, circled his thumb on her clit and she exploded. He licked her gently until she stopped clenching around him, then crawled back up her body and kissed her again.

She tasted herself on him, nearly cried at the gentle kiss he gave her this time, shocked by the gratitude he showed. He was the one who'd pleasured her but he acted as though she'd given him a great gift. He pulled away with a last gentle nip and said, "Again."

She couldn't speak as he made the journey south again, once more spending what felt like hours on her breasts. He was gentle with one, cupping it lovingly, brushing the nipple softly, while he savaged the other with lips, tongue and teeth.

Then he switched and Hillary realized that the first orgasm, which had seemed so incredible, was going to be nothing compared to the next. Already she was panting hard, her head moving from side to side as she tried to ease the tension building higher and higher. This time he let his hands move to her pussy while his mouth stayed to tend to her breasts.

One long finger entered her gently and her hips bucked up to meet it, her inner walls clenching desperately to hold him, any part of him, in her. He groaned around one nipple, then moved back up to kiss her mouth, no longer sweet and gentle, while he pushed another finger into her and brushed his thumb across her clit. His tongue fucked her mouth in time with his finger. The wave of pleasure burst through Hillary and she cried out, collapsing back to the bed, spent.

Or so she thought. She moaned as Zach removed his hand, then moaned again as he lowered his body to hers. She delighted in the feel of his weight on her, his chest rubbing her nipples, his thighs heavy against hers. He kissed her nose, then the corner of each eye, and then looked at her.

"Please, Zach, I'll do anything you want, just get inside me, please." Her grip on the headboard was so tight she worried she might break it.

"Touch me," was all he said, as he slid his arms under her, hooking his hands around her shoulders. She didn't hesitate, putting her arms to his back, holding him as close as he would allow. Their gazes locked, he entered her in one smooth move.

She was tight but wet, her body anxious to receive him. She felt the resurgence of her power, which had been lying quietly in wait. Now her wolf and her power surged forward to meet Zach's, and the meeting was so sublime it nearly eclipsed the pleasure she felt at his being seated within her.

"Holy hell," he said, not moving. "Do you feel that?"

She nodded. They could feel their separate powers twining together, feel their wolves rubbing against each other, feel their souls binding.

"Oh baby, thank God I found you." Zach kissed the tears from her eyes.

"I love you, Zach."

His eyes closed as if in prayer, and a tear fell. Then he began to move. The feeling of him moving inside her, pushing roughly against her walls, finding spots inside her that she'd never guessed at, put her over the edge. There was no buildup, just an insane burst of pleasure that left her boneless, barely able to hang on as Zach roared, flooding her with his seed.

He collapsed on top of her then rolled to his side, bringing her with him. She was so exhausted, so replete that it took her a minute to realize he was speaking. He was kissing her hair, her eyes, her cheeks, saying, "I love you, I love you, I love you." She drifted to sleep, her smile smug with intense satisfaction.

Hours later Hillary woke to the delicious pleasure of Zach leaning over her, his face inches from hers as he watched her response to what his fingers were doing, moving gently in and out of her pussy and around her clit. Her back arched and she gasped. He leaned down and kissed her, gently, sweetly. *Mmm. So this is what love tastes like.* He pulled back just far enough to whisper, "Mine."

She erupted at the word, using her hands to hold him to her as if he had any intention of getting away. Finally she pulled him back, gasping for air. He rolled to his back, bringing her with him and setting her on his cock in one smooth thrust. She gasped again, placing her hands on his chest for support.

Zachary's hands found her breasts as he nudged his hips up in a not so subtle invitation. She tensed her thighs, arching her back to get just the right angle and began to ride him. She pulled his hands from her chest and linked their fingers, using his strength to help drive her onto his shaft. The pleasure was incredible, and while part of her longed to make it last, she was unable to resist the rising need. She looked down at him, hoping he was as close as she was.

His eyes were closed tight as he fought to control himself. She gave his hand an extra squeeze and he opened his eyes. Their gazes locked, he pushed himself up while she slammed herself down and they both came, hard and fast, unable to look away. Collapsing on top of him, Hillary told him she loved him and fell fast asleep, his arms tight around her, her pussy still holding him inside.

The next time they woke, Hillary was on her stomach, halfway on top of Zach, one of his legs between hers and his hand cupped possessively around the nape of her neck. She moaned lightly, feeling so pleasantly sore, not wanting to move a muscle. His thumb caressed her neck gently and he kissed her shoulder. They lay like that for a few minutes, until she turned over and snuggled into him.

"It was hard for me to imagine, when I read the information about mates, how it would really be. I found the idea of being bound together without conscious choice terrifying. When I met you, and could feel something happening inside, I was scared, my brain telling me to run, but really, it was all so simple."

Zach grunted at that, causing her to laugh slightly but also to caress his side soothingly .

"No, that's not what I mean. I know it was hard for you to be so gentle and patient, and it was terrifying for me to deal with the whole werewolf thing, and the pack. It still is. But you. That part was easy no matter how much I tried to use logic to tell myself otherwise. You're just...mine." Her breath left her as he squeezed her tightly to him.

"I knew and believed the stories of mates. I've seen it plenty of times, seen the way my parents are with each other, watched as Aaron and Tracy, and other wolves mated.

Still, I was completely unprepared for meeting you. You are totally amazing and I feel like the luckiest guy in the world." He propped himself up against the headboard, and she sat up, watching him.

"I want you to know that I understand you might not consider us married, as my culture does. It's probably too early to ask you to marry me, by your standards, but I will anyway. I love you and I want to commit myself to you in every way that matters to both of us. If you need more time to get to know me, I'll understand, but I can't not ask you to pledge yourself to me and let me do the same."

Hillary's eyes were wide as she watched him, saw how deeply he meant what he said. Part of her still reeled at the idea that this man she'd met only days before, this wolf who could clearly be so dangerous was already tied to her soul. There was no denying the truth of it though. Still, she was a product of her culture, and felt that she would never be wholly comfortable if she didn't have a wedding of some sort.

"Tell me, please, what you're thinking. I can handle anything as long as I know what you're thinking," he said, reaching out to trace his fingers over her cheek.

"I was thinking that on the one hand, of course I feel what you're feeling, that we're tied together at the soul. It's beautiful and I'm so blessed to have that with you. On the other hand, I would like some kind of wedding. It doesn't have to be fancy or anything. I don't have family to do up a big event. Maybe just at the courthouse in Slade, if you don't mind. A couple of friends. Soon."

"Thank God," he said, grabbing her up for another kiss. Hillary pushed him back.

"You said I could have a turn, and I still haven't gotten to explore you." She pushed hard to get him to lie back against the headboard again. She kissed him some more before leaving his mouth to trail kisses down his chin. She spent some time at the hollow of his neck, while his hands stroked her back and their breathing increased.

His thumbs began to caress her breasts and she sat back. "Uh-uh, my turn. If you touch me there I won't be able to stand it." He put his hands back on the bed and she continued her journey. She decided to give his nipples the same treatment he had hers. She sucked one while pinching the other in rhythm. He groaned, his hands fisting in the sheets to keep himself still.

Hillary sat up so that she could see the magnificent body spread out before her. His stomach was tan and tight, and resting against it was his penis, reaching up toward her. Her curiosity got the best of her and she reached for him, not planning on pleasure, only wanting to explore. She ran her fingers over the head, delighted that it produced a drop of moisture at the slit. She used her fingers to test it, feel it.

ZACH WAS HAVING a hell of a time keeping his word to stay still and let Hillary explore his body. When she put her finger to her tongue to see what he tasted like, he lost it.

He surged up, grabbing her and twisting her beneath him. He nudged her legs open with his and brought the head of his cock to her pussy. He barely managed to wait, putting his fingers where his dick wanted to go, testing her. He sighed with relief to find her wet and waiting, and plunged in.

He tried to slow down but she wrapped her legs around him, heels digging into his ass, hips thrusting up to meet him, stroke for stroke. Damn, he needed control. He bit her earlobe but that caused her to clench tighter around him. Gritting his teeth, he propped up on his elbows, using both hands to smooth the hair back from her face. Her eyes were glazed with passion and it took her a second to meet his eyes, really see him. When she did, she brought her hands up to frame his face too.

"You are so incredible," he whispered, pleased when she didn't shake off his compliment. "Gorgeous and sexy and *hot*." He drew the words out, giving one long, deliberate push into her with each one. Her legs dropped from his ass, letting him set the pace he needed. The way she gave herself to him tightened his throat.

"You're pretty hot yourself," she said, ending with a gasp as he pressed his groin against her clit. Her eyes started to close.

"Stay with me. I'm not ready to leave you yet. I love being here, inside you, with you. Completely."

She focused on him again, ran her hands through his hair, clenching them in time with his movements. Every catch of her breath, every tiny whimper and shuddering sigh were music to his ears. As sweet as the screams he had coaxed from her earlier, and when she had shouted his name.

Her pussy fluttered around him and he stilled, letting the sensation work its way through him. As her orgasm slowly built, he settled his lips over hers and began to move again, long, slow strokes that took all of his concentration. His hands fisted the bedding beside her head and her legs came back up around him, urging him on, harder, faster. He increased his pace, each stroke harder than the last as she began to cry out her release into his feasting mouth. Finally he couldn't hold it back any longer. She sucked on his tongue and he ground into her, giving in to the release. The orgasm felt as if it came all the way from his toes, draining every last molecule of energy from him.

He collapsed on top of her, Hillary stroking his back. He was glad that she could still move, but worried she might be having a hard time breathing, so he gathered what scraps of energy he could and rolled to the side.

"You okay?" he couldn't keep himself from asking.

Her mouth quirked up and if he'd had the strength he'd give it a little bite.

"Wouldn't you know if I wasn't?"

"Smart ass. Yes, I guess I would, but that doesn't mean I don't want to double- and triple-check. I've never had a mate before, you know."

She rolled her eyes at him. "I'm fine. I'm better than fine. I didn't even know there was such a thing as being as fantastic as I am right now. I thought it was a myth, kind of like werewolves."

He smiled at her. "I've often wondered if there were vampires or other werecreatures out there."

"Don't you think you would know?"

"Probably."

They lay for a time, quiet. Finally he thought he could stand without wobbling and got off the bed.

"I'll be right back," he said, over his shoulder. "Don't move."

He returned quickly with their bags and dropped them on the floor. Drawing her to the edge of the bed, he knelt in front of her and pulled out the ring box he'd stuffed into his pocket. He prayed she'd like the ring. With only a few hours to get to the city and shop, and having known her for such a short time, he'd worried that he wouldn't be able to find something she might like. The minute he'd seen the diamond flanked by sapphires he'd known it was her. Now that it was too late, chilly sweat rolled down his spine.

"Will you marry me, Hillary Abbott?" he asked, slipping the ring onto her shaking finger.

Hillary slid off the bed onto his thighs, wrapping her arms around him and hugging him tight.

"Yes, Zach, you're mine now and I won't let you get away." She grinned at him. Then she looked over his shoulder at her hand.

"Oh," she gasped. "Oh Zach, it's really beautiful."

"I hope you like it. I didn't have a lot of time to pick it out. I didn't want to be away too long in case you needed me, but I had to go to the city to find you something special. I know I haven't really had time to get to know your tastes, so if it's not right, I won't be hurt if you want to go with me, get something different."

She curled her hand into a fist and glared at him. "You are *not* touching this ring!"

Relief made him giddy and he was probably grinning like a fool when he picked her up and swung her around.

CHAPTER SIX

After breakfast they went for a run. Hillary could hardly wait to see Zach as a wolf. They left their clothes in the cabin and walked outside, hand in hand. Hillary felt extra naked without the ring she'd worn for only a couple of hours. How had she become a sentimental fool so quickly?

Zach kissed her, stepped back and became wolf. Hillary kneeled and plunged her hands into the gorgeous gray pelt, shot through with black. His gray eyes were on her face and he licked her cheek. She laughed and hugged him before standing up and changing shape.

Becoming wolf was easy, she had only to let go of her human shape, let the wolf take over. It was always ready and waiting, wanting its chance to run free. Zach came to her immediately, sniffing her all over, and Hillary did the same. She was once again amazed at how important what she smelled was. She smelled mate and pack and she could swear she smelled love. They sat for a time, rubbing each other, then Hillary nipped him in challenge and took off running.

They ran for hours, catching a couple of rabbits for lunch. She shouldn't have been shocked to become aroused, running and playing with Zach, but she was. She'd never had any kind of sex thoughts as a wolf, but now her wolf had a mate and it wasn't long before she was teasing him, lifting her tail in front of him then dashing off when he got close. She enjoyed playing with him until suddenly, with no warning, she was done playing. She didn't want him holding back, letting her get away. Denying her his strength. She gave a tiny growl and his hackles rose. His wagging tail stilled and the power of who he was rose up around him. Her wolf rejoiced. This was her mate, her alpha. Their eyes met, a split second of awareness before she turned and raced away.

No longer teasing, she gave everything she had into getting away. If he couldn't catch her, he didn't deserve to have her. A long howl broke through the still forest and a shiver of need prickled through her. He was coming.

Instinct had her breaking hard to the right just in time to avoid being tackled, but it only saved her a second's freedom. Spinning as he landed, Zach surged forward, catching her back legs, tripping them both into a tumbling pile. She scrambled to get her feet under her, almost managed it before his full weight pinned her down. A low growl came from her throat, sounding threatening despite the way her heart pounded in anticipation. But he knew. He answered her challenge by locking his jaws on her shoulder and biting down. Not hard enough to damage, not hard enough to hurt, not really. But she felt it. Sensation shuddered through her whole body as she gave in to him. He mounted her in one swift movement, and before she had a thought to react, he entered her.

More, harder, faster. She couldn't say the words, but she knew just how to make sure Zach knew what she wanted. She let loose the whine that was trapped in her throat. At the same time, she bucked and wiggled, just enough to remind Zach that he better hold on. He more than held on. He unleashed his control and pounded into her, his jaw tightening against her flesh. She howled her completion and every muscle in her body went limp as Zach came hard. His penis knotted inside her, a completely foreign sensation that her wolf expected and welcomed. He lay on top of her, giving licks to her muzzle and answering her small whines with nips to her neck. She had never felt so safe, so comforted.

At some point his cock slipped free and they rose to find the stream. She was desperately thirsty after all their hard work. When Zach was drinking, she playfully bumped him into the stream, making him splash about to catch himself. He turned on her, a look of canine disgust that had her tongue hanging out in silent laughter.

They napped in the sun until it started to go down, then made their way back to the cabin more slowly, enjoying the woods together. When they got back, Hillary would have changed but Zach nudged her into the cabin and up the stairs. He led her to the mirrored closet doors and they sat together. Zach's dark gray fur with black highlights looked beautiful next to her plain white fur, she thought. He licked her muzzle and changed. She let him pet her for a few minutes then changed too.

They cooked dinner, laughing and touching constantly. The conversation covered distant things, the country, the world, TV shows and books, nothing that hit too close to home. They worked together in the kitchen easily, their skills complementing each other.

AFTER DINNER, Zach went to the fireplace in the living room to get it started and Hillary pulled the blanket from the back of the couch, settling into it while she watched him work. This day of peace had centered her, helped her to regain the balance she had lost since meeting Aaron, he could tell. Every moment that passed she settled more and more comfortably into herself. He joined her on the couch and they snuggled close, Hillary practically sitting on his lap. They remained quiet for a few minutes, Zach caressing her hand, bringing the ring to his lips for a kiss. He looked at her, getting serious, but she spoke first.

"I know you want to deal with my past, do something to make them pay. But right now I feel like I need to focus on getting my footing with the pack. I don't know if you can understand, but that part, having a pack, I mean, is still very scary for me, and I *hate* being scared." She laid her head against his shoulder, her hand on his arm, needing the touch of his skin.

Zach placed a kiss on her forehead. "I do understand that it's scary for you, it's a huge unknown. The only experience you have with pack until us was terrifying and evil. How could you not be scared? I understand that, but I also know that when you meet the pack it will be no different than when you met Aaron and Tracy and me. Except that you'll at least be aware of the fact that all were-wolves are not like those disgusting shits you met, and that the three of us are your friends and will be at your side the whole way."

"But that might not be true, Zach. I've only been around the three of you a bit and already I understand that pack loyalty is a very strong force. What if there comes a time, a situation, where you have to choose between us? I think the incredible loyalty that's natural to the pack must be how that other pack got so evil. How else can you explain the whole pack?"

He tried to figure out how to explain something that just *was*, something he never needed to think about, let alone express. "You're right that the instinct toward loyalty is very strong and most certainly played a part in how they came to be the way that they are. There is a magic to being a werewolf, something that defies science and logic, and usually keeps us grounded and together. It's how mates come together and how alphas are born. It's why there are rarely fights for dominance in a culture that you would think would demand them on a regular basis." He brought his hand up to her neck, tickling along her hairline, winning a small sigh from her.

"The instincts are deeper than just pack, though they generally encompass all werewolf kind. You're a very strong alpha in your own right, so you haven't felt the pull to...not just obey, but support, I guess you could say, an alpha. When you meet an alpha who is more powerful than you, you'll see what I mean, although, to tell you the truth, there aren't many who would be more powerful than us."

He moved his hand back to her shoulder so he wouldn't get too excited and she smiled, snuggling into him.

"Plus, now that we're mated, our power will increase. Mated pairs in the hierarchy are always more powerful than when they were single. It doesn't necessarily mean you jump a level, but it means you might be more powerful than a single wolf you used to be equal to. It will be interesting to see how we compare with those who were my equals before.

"It goes the other way, too, which you've felt. Being alpha isn't like being elected president. It's something you *have* to do, if you're the alpha. You don't choose it, it chooses you. When you met Aaron, you must have felt scared. And yet, you felt his submission to you before he displayed it. You were afraid, but not really afraid *of him*. You knew he could change and attack you, and probably felt you could take him, but it still would have been a battle and you could have been hurt. Did that scare you?"

"No, it was more the fear that there were more of him, that they'd found me and would come and get me. I was determined to fight to the death, no matter how many of them tried to subdue me." He squeezed her tightly but she didn't feel distressed. Instead she put her hand on his cheek and soothed *him*.

"But I see what you mean. I could tell that he was strong, but not as strong as me. And when he met me in the woods, after I'd had a chance to push the initial fears aside, I could sense that he meant me no harm, that he was determined but not pushing for a fight."

He stroked his hand down her arm. "Then when you met the three of us at the restaurant, how did you react to Aaron and Tracy?"

"I thought I would be afraid to be with three of you at once, but I felt...I don't know, it's hard to describe. By the time we were wolves in the woods, I felt protective. Even though I knew that they were keeping close to protect me, both physically and from my fears about being out of control, I felt protective toward them, like they were mine and it was important that I take care of them."

"That's exactly what I mean," Zach confirmed. "When you're in the hierarchy of a pack, but most especially when you're an alpha, it's not just logically that you feel you must care for and support your pack, it's internally, a driving need. When something goes wrong with one of my wolves, I know it. I know who's in trouble and if the need is strong enough I can even track them down. When Aaron mated with Tracy I was still the first, but when my sister Molly mated with her husband Travis last year, I felt it. It was pretty amazing, feeling their souls come together, even from a distance."

"Wow," Hillary breathed. "This whole pack thing is pretty intense."

"Yes," Zach agreed. "But what I'm trying to point out is that in its own way, the feeling of pack and loyalty and being pack alpha, which you now are, is as natural as the mating was. Just like it was hard for you to comprehend until you experienced it, when you meet the pack I think it'll all fall into place. It's already starting, really. Inside you're making connections through me. I think it'll just be pretty subtle until you actually meet them. I bet if something happened to one of the members right now, you would feel it. I guarantee you would if it were Aaron or Tracy."

"I never wanted to be in charge of other people. Stephen had to beg me to let him work with me, to teach him what I do."

"And once he was there?"

Hillary sighed. "I couldn't remember what it was like to not have him around. He's a good guy." She paused. "I guess I'm going to have to give up the shop," she said.

Zach laid his head back against the couch, feeling guilty. "I'm sorry, baby, I wish it were just a little bit closer. We can move, it's not like we're tied to my house, but we need to stay within a certain distance of the pack house and that's just a bit too far to commute to Slade. You don't need to make any decisions until you see Mountain View. I'm embarrassed to say I don't really know what you do enough to tell you if there's already something like that there." He frowned. "Aaron never did tell me what kind of shop you had, only that he met you there." He raised his brow at her.

"Um. Right. Well, I'll need to talk to Aaron a little bit before I explain more about that." His eyebrows shot up, in surprise this time.

"Okaaaay," he drawled out, then remembered what they had been talking about. "Anyway, what I was trying to say was that I know you're worried about meeting the pack, and I totally respect that. I just think that once you do, it will take you no time at all to get settled in. In the meantime, the thought of what those sick excuses for wolves might be doing to other women is just about killing me."

Zach cursed his stupidity as Hillary's face lost all color.

"Oh shit, Zach, oh shit. I never thought about it like that, I swear I didn't! What if...how many..." She jumped off his lap and ran for the bathroom. He was right behind her, catching her hair as she bent over the toilet, vomiting her dinner. He held her hair and rubbed her back until she finally ceased. She sat back and he got her some water. She looked as if she were in shock, her eyes glassy and unfocused. He made her swish some water and spit it out, then picked her up and carried her back to the couch. Damn, he was an insensitive idiot.

As he sat down, he felt her rein in her focus. She turned anguished eyes up at him and he wished he could take his careless words back.

"What have I done? Four years, Zach, four years..." she trailed off, horror written all over her face.

"Stop that," he ordered sharply. "You will *not* blame yourself for this. You did what was necessary to survive, to heal, to move on. Even if you had thought about it, what could you have done? You had nobody to turn to, and you certainly weren't in any shape to take them on by yourself."

"I could have called the police, made a statement, or maybe an anonymous tip. I don't know! I didn't even try." She tried to hide her head in his shoulder, but he gripped her chin, brought her eyes to his.

"I won't have this, Hillary, I *will not*. You did nothing wrong." He said it with power so that she would know, would feel, the strength of his belief in the statement. In her. She didn't look completely convinced but she squared her shoulders.

"Okay, Zach. What do we do?" He rewarded her for listening to him and using that "we" without a moment's thought, by kissing her gently and hugging her tightly. He stood up from the couch, still holding her, and walked to the kitchen. He sat her on the counter while he rummaged through the cupboards, pulling out two glasses and a bottle of scotch. He poured them each a drink, handed both glasses to her and carried her back to the couch. He set her down, stoked the fire, and returned to her.

"You need to tell me all of it. Everything you can remember."

Hillary took a deep breath, and a small swallow of her drink. She stiffened her spine and told him.

By the time she had finished, Zachary had finished his drink and hers. Only his determination to show her that he could be as strong as her, a worthy mate to her, gave him the will to hold his power in check, to push back the need to rage and storm.

"I guess now, when I look back, some of the things they said make sense, but at the time it was so confusing."

She looked up at him and her eyes softened. She put her hand on his cheek, gave him a kiss, comforting him. God, he so did not deserve her.

"I need to finish this, Zach. I don't think I'll be able to do it again." She turned so that her back was to his front, her legs between his. He wrapped his arms securely around her, drawing strength as well as giving it.

"Just before the attack, Jeff definitely called his uncle, Ken Cage, 'Alpha'. And when he was introducing me around, it was a bit more possessive than he'd been when we were in school, which was making me uncomfortable. Of course, I just put it off to introducing the girlfriend to family.

"I can see now that Jeff was bringing me home for the approval of the pack, of the alpha. He was surprised when his mother said they would be doing the bonfire that night. I think he thought this trip was just introductory and that he was getting permission to keep seeing me, not to bring me in. But once she said that, probably on approval from Ken now that I think about it, he was excited. That was part of what was making me nervous, the way he was acting, the way people were looking at me, wondering if I would survive the change, I guess." She looked back at him. "Tell me about werewolf attacks, about changing a human to a werewolf. I read a bit on the website but there wasn't a lot there."

"That's because it is so rare, so prohibited. Most of the time, unless there are serious extenuating circumstances, the penalty for attacking a human while in werewolf form is execution. That's one of two ways to change a human, to attack them while you're in werewolf form. You saw that we have two forms we can change into, the full wolf, and the wolf-man from horror movies. A bite from the full wolf would be no different than the bite from a regular wolf, but the bite from the werewolf form is like a virus. Most of the time it's fatal, but occasionally it converts the human to one of us." He shuddered. "I haven't even heard of it happening in my lifetime. When changing, you have to make a very conscious decision to only change partway, so even if provoked or in extreme danger, it would be rare to not change fully into wolf to attack or defend ourselves. It's just the more natural inclination."

She looked thoughtful. "Only Jeff changed like that, everyone else changed to wolf. Why is it so fatal?"

"I don't know," he shrugged. "Part of the magic, I guess. Maybe to keep some psycho from finding a bunch of psycho friends and changing them? Population control?"

"What's the other kind of change?" she asked. "You said there were two."

"Once in a while a werewolf will sense their mate in a human. They're required to introduce the human to their alpha..." He trailed off, remembering her story, trying to figure out what the idiots had been thinking. "They have to introduce the human to their alpha, who can use his or her tie to the wolf to examine the link, and see if the bond really exists, or if the wolf is just a bit overeager. If the alpha agrees, then they help the wolf explain the situation to the human.

"If a couple is a mated pair, the werewolf bites their mate while having sex, in human form. Not a mauling bite, but a mating bite like a natural wolf will give his mate while mounting her—on the shoulder. It triggers the mate bond. It doesn't work if the pair isn't mated. It's possible, though I've never heard it tried, that you don't actually have to be having sex. But really, who wants to get bitten if they're not distracted by sex?"

"Hmph."

"When the human is changed, it's the alpha's responsibility to see that they're part of a pack and that they understand the laws. If the human freaks when told, the alpha is responsible for doing what they can to control the situation."

"Which means...?" Hillary asked testily.

He smiled at her protectiveness. She was so born to be an alpha. "It's hard to say, it depends on the situation. It's not happened in our pack since I was alpha. You have to remember, if the bond is true, if they really are mates, the magic is working on the human too, and as surprised or freaked out as they might be, they're feeling the pull toward their mate as well."

She stayed quiet, thinking it through. Then relaxed back against him. "Well, I suppose if the magic could get me into your bed this quickly, then it can help a human deal with the shock of finding out their lover's a werewolf."

"Exactly." He knew he sounded smug when she elbowed him in the ribs. "The werewolf and human must have sex before meeting the alpha. That makes it easier to sense the bond. I know an alpha in Florida who had a hard time because one of his wolves fell in love with a Catholic girl, who was determined to hold her virginity to the marriage bed. The wolf was totally convinced that she was his mate, but the alpha didn't think so. He was worried that he just wasn't sensing it because they hadn't had sex. Finally he told the wolf he had to leave the area for thirty days and if, when he came back, he was still sure of the bond, the alpha would reconsider. The wolf went to another pack to drown his sorrow and complain about his alpha and fell in love with a wolf in that pack. They were mated before the first week was up."

Hillary laughed. "Tell me another happy story before I finish."

"There are gay wolves, you know. It's not as common with wolves as with humans, so there's a higher percentage of them finding their mates with humans. When Samuel was alpha, our second, Alex Knight, came to us from the Midwest to see if he fit into our pack and our hierarchy. He fit well and became our third. We had one gay wolf in the pack. He took one look at Alex and about shit his pants, then ran out to the nearest gay bar. He was so not at Alex's level and he knew it, and told me later that the idea of being around that much stud and not being able to touch would drive him crazy." Zach chuckled at the memory.

"Anyway, the closest gay bar was not extremely close and Uncle Sam got a frantic call at three in the morning, insisting that the alpha come and meet his mate. This was only a couple of years ago, and Sam was giving serious consideration to retiring, so I'm sure he wasn't thrilled, but Tommy was very insistent. The guy lived in New York and was just passing through town, so it had to be done that night.

"It was nearly four by the time Sam got there. He told me that he could smell sex and feel the lust and excitement, and even though we're not the homophobic prudes many humans are, he wasn't exactly anxious to go inside. The door opened and there was this biker guy, full leathers and chains, and little Tommy tied to the bed inside." Hillary jerked slightly at the mention of the bonds and he rubbed his hands up and down her arms to soothe her.

"Uncle Sam started to get defensive, thinking Tommy had been attacked. I don't know what Tommy said to calm Uncle Sam down, but it turned out that Tommy was a submissive and this guy was a Dom. Tommy had let the guy think that he belonged to Uncle Sam, figuring that was the easiest way to get Sam into the picture."

"Oh my."

"Sam said the bond was pretty strong for a regular wolf, he had no doubt they were mates. So Bob was feeling very possessive already. Sam held up his hands and said, 'He's all yours if he wants you, but you have to untie him for a few minutes. I have to make sure he wants to go with you.' Bob untied Tommy, who was thrilled until Sam gave him a look and he realized he was going to have to explain about being a werewolf.

"In the end, Sam had to be the one to explain it and to make the change so Bob could see that Sam and Tommy were telling the truth. Bob agreed to stay in town for a couple of weeks to get used to the change and for Sam to talk to the alpha in New York and start the petition for their joining that pack."

She smiled up at him then took a deep breath, her face becoming serious. "I guess, now that I know what I do, Jeff thought I was his mate. But Ken should have known better." She looked at him for confirmation and he nodded. "So he was willing to do it anyway, let Jeff attack me..." She trailed off, giving him a look of confusion.

Zach propped his chin on top of Hillary's head. "I think that, most likely, they hoped you would survive, but didn't really think you would. The whole thing, in addition to being evil, is really odd. I mean, it's not a secret how to go about it, what it feels like to meet your mate. As I recall, Uncle Sam was only called on to meet a human mate twice, and both times the wolf was right. Usually when you hear the stories about the human not being a mate, the wolf is very young and eager, not experienced enough to feel the difference between lust and love."

"I don't know if it makes it better or worse that they were crazy stupid on top of being evil. Delusional I guess is better than genius, when it comes to that sort of thing."

He grunted an agreement.

"Anyway," she continued. "The bonfire and attack were the night we got there, then they raped me on and off the next few days. The night of the full moon they dragged me from the room and changed into wolves. I was mostly out of it, freaked out when they would come up to me, push at me, or bite at me. It seems as if they were genuinely waiting to see if I would change. Ken was the last to

change, then he looked at me for a bit and ran off with the others."
She paused then rushed through the rest.

"All that time, I was hurting and trying to stay conscious, trying to figure out what I should do, what I *could* do. I was so angry that I was just lying there unable to do anything. I felt *something*. Now I realize it was the moon and the power coming into me, but at the time it just scared me and I pushed it away, like I was pushing the pain away. It hurt to push it away, and that just pissed me off and made me more determined not to give in to it, sure that it was a bad thing." She got up and paced the room.

Zach forced himself to stay still, letting her get it all out.

"When I finally changed, I was freaked, yes, but also felt amazingly better. I was sore and my body ached, but I wasn't *hurt* anymore. I was exhausted, but I could run, so I did. I ran for hours, and I know that they chased me once they realized I'd changed and gone. I went away from the city, afraid of what would happen if I saw people, of what I might do, afraid of leading the wolves to other people. I made it to a forest, which sort of surprised me as I'd been in a desert, and crashed. I slept the day away and just kept moving from that point on. I think it was probably a week before I decided to change back and try to get to a town.

"It had been easier to eat and stay warm as the wolf and I guess I just wasn't ready to deal with what had happened yet. I was also afraid to try to turn back and not be able to, which sounds pretty stupid now, but I wasn't feeling very rational at that point. I found some hikers and tracked their scent back to their campsite, finding it empty. I stole some clothes and went into town. I went to the bank and told them I had just come from the police station to report a mugging, and that I had lost everything. It took a while for them to contact my bank and verify everything, but I got some money. I never went back to Los Angeles. I was too afraid."

She finally turned to face him. He came to her and hugged her, not saying anything for a while, just needing to hold her. Finally, he leaned back so he could see her face. "You are amazing and I am so damn proud that you're my mate. You're strong and courageous and one seriously badass wolf, and you don't even know it."

He went to a pack he'd left in the living room the previous night and pulled out his laptop. He opened it and turned it on, walking to the kitchen table to set it down.

"The website that Aaron told you about, I'm sure you looked around a bit?" he asked while the computer whirred into activity.

"Yes, I can't believe there's all that information on there." She laughed and shook her head.

"There's a different section for the hierarchies. We can find out information about other packs. It makes things a lot easier than they used to be."

Once the computer was booted, he opened the browser and clicked on his link to the website. He typed *Miami, Florida*, and hit enter so she could see the type of information that came up. It told the name of the alpha and the range of his territory. It showed the pack's basic territory, as well as the surrounding areas that they were responsible for, though no pack lived there.

"That's why when Aaron met you he was upset to find a rogue wolf living in our territory without our knowledge. There are wolves who prefer to live on their own, not in a pack. That's fine, as long as they follow the laws, which are mostly about the safety of, and secrecy from, humans. Wolves are supposed to contact the pack, usually the fourth, when they plan on coming through a territory, even if they're not staying. If they're vacationing, they'll usually come visit the pack, stay at or near the pack house. If they're just doing the tourist thing, or have no interest in hanging out with the local wolves, they're still required to let the pack know where, in general, they'll be, for how long, how they can be contacted, that kind of thing.

"If a wolf wants to move to the territory, but not be part of the pack, they technically have to ask permission. An alpha would need a really good reason to deny permission and then the wolf could apply to the national council for a decision if they weren't happy with the alpha's. It's not very common for wolves to live outside of a pack, so it's very rare for this to happen."

He went back to the initial search screen and typed *Phoenix, Arizona,* and hit enter. The alphas whose names came up were William and Janet Sanderson. The map showed that while their area was all of Arizona and half of New Mexico, the pack actually resided in Tucson, in the southeast corner of the state, about a hundred miles away from Phoenix.

"Why are the areas so big? How can anyone be expected to control such a large expanse?" Hillary asked.

"It's not usually a problem. There aren't enough wolves, enough packs, to be less spread out, and for the most part that's a good thing. Like I said, most wolves live with one of the packs, and if they get into trouble, they do it there, not a hundred miles away."

They searched through the information and found the Cages, Ken, John, Shannon and Jeff on the membership, but no mention of them living in Phoenix.

"We need to contact the National Council secretary. I think right now that's Tom Engles in Chicago. He can tell us who we should contact, or if the council should convene to discuss this. Most likely he'll pass it on straight to the president, since this is so serious."

"Explain the president bit to me."

"The first or second of every pack is allowed to be a member of the national council. Basically, if the pack is particularly powerful, like ours, you're supposed to send your second, so that the council members are more or less equal in terms of power. They divide up into committees to work on problems and get together to vote on decisions. The top ten most powerful packs in the country have a conclave once a year to elect a National Alpha." He studiously ignored her quirked eyebrow, pretending he didn't know the question that she wasn't asking.

"It's really mostly an honorific, because it's rare for something to happen that the council can't see to and enforce on their own. I think the last time the president was called on to act was three years ago, when some nutcase in Atlanta found out about werewolves and went hunting. The council made the decision to execute the human after he'd shot and killed three innocent werewolves, as well as five natural wolves. Even though the council made the decision, it was generally agreed that the president should be the one to actually carry out the action." He gave a slight shudder. "Thankfully those kinds of actions are rarely required."

She gave him an exasperated look.

He gave her a quick kiss but she didn't open her mouth so he relented.

"Yes, our pack has a history of its alphas being elected to National Council President. Uncle Sam was president six times in his thirty years as alpha. You have to be alpha for at least five years before you're considered for the voting."

She grinned at him. "You are so going to be president one day."

He smirked at her and pointed out, "You're pack alpha now, too, sweetie. You'll be just as eligible in five years." He laughed as her grin fell away and she wrinkled her nose.

Enough serious business. Zachary stood and pulled Hillary to her feet. He put his shoulder to her waist and hoisted her up, bounding up the stairs while she squawked indignantly. She swatted his butt and he gave it an extra wiggle for her. He bounced her onto the bed and she immediately rolled to get off on the other side. Zachary leapt on top of her, so she changed tactics and pushed off backward. He fell off the bed, but took her with him, rolling after he hit the floor, so that he was on top.

He looked down at her laughing face. He knew she wasn't scared, but, well...

HILLARY FELT ZACH tense slightly after they landed on the floor. She looked in his eyes and could see nervousness creep in. She reached both hands up to cup his face. "Nothing you could do would ever remind me of that day, those men. Please don't ever treat me carefully, or delicately. I like that you see me as a strong woman."

She lifted up to kiss him gently, playing with his lips, which he kept closed. She moved one hand down his shoulder to his arm then pinched him. When he opened his mouth to complain, she thrust her tongue in, although it was hard because she was trying not to laugh.

Zachary growled, although she could see him fighting off a smile as well. He pushed her back down to the floor and grabbed her wrists, holding them above her head. He pressed down on them for a moment, letting her know he wanted her to keep them there. Then he trailed his hands down her arms, tickling her gently on the sensitive underside. He brought his hands down her sides, to the hem of her shirt.

Hillary moaned as he reversed direction, taking the shirt with him. He slid his hands up her rib cage, finally pulling the shirt over her head, letting go of their kiss while she lifted her head. He left the shirt tangled in her hands then began the journey south once again. This time he detoured to her breasts and Hillary arched her back, wanting more, needing more.

"You are so exquisite," he muttered, sitting back on his heels to look at her. His thumbs teased her nipples, flicking them back and forth, back and forth. Suddenly he pinched them and she shrieked at the pleasure and pain of it. He pulled on them gently, then bent down and laved first one then the other with his tongue.

They were both breathing hard. Hillary was rocking her hips, trying to relieve the ache that was building, but he denied her. "No, I want more of these breasts, I love these breasts." He fitted his mouth over one, taking most of it in, biting very gently, sucking hard. "I think we should get you some jewelry for these," he said, sitting up again to look at what his work had accomplished. She opened her eyes and saw him looking at her and she felt beautiful.

"Please, Zachary, I want to touch you. I want to kiss you all over. I want to play with your nipples and explore your cock. I never got my turn."

His hands never stopped moving on her breasts. "I know, baby,

I'm sorry. I'm sure I'll be able to control myself after we do this another...hundred times or so. Then I'm all yours."

Finally, he began moving downward, reaching her jeans with his hands while his mouth came back down to play with her nipples. He undid her jeans and shoved them down her hips, lifting off her to pull them all the way down, then removed his own jeans and his shirt.

Hillary almost wept as he brought his hands to her feet, clearly planning to resume his investigation of her body from the bottom up this time. He kissed her foot, nipped her anklebone when she growled at him. His hands reached up to her thighs to hold her still while his mouth meandered its way up her legs, alternating between the two. He spread her legs wide so that he could get to the backs of her knees, licking and nibbling for what felt like hours, before moving on. It was worse this time, knowing what was coming, anticipating what he would do, but having to wait.

Hillary's head was already thrashing back and forth by the time he reached her upper thigh, his shoulders forcing her legs wide. Like the night before, he paused, looking at her. She could feel his warm breath on her curls. All thought left her as he began to explore her with his tongue, lips and teeth.

Zach licked up one side and then the other. He found her entrance and fluttered his tongue at the rim before thrusting inside. He licked and nipped and soothed and sucked, everywhere but her clit. Hillary was moaning continuously now, begging him to fuck her. Then he brought his fingers into play. He tickled her pussy, brushed through her curls, and at last put one finger into her, slowly, oh so slowly. He wiggled it around, exploring her walls, hooking it just so until she jumped under him. Then he added another finger.

Hillary came hard and fast, fluttering around Zach's fingers, clutching them tight. Just as she was coming down, ready to collapse, boneless, he fused his mouth to her clit. Immediately she was back on the edge. She felt him drawing her cream from her body, while his mouth did delicious things to her clit. Then she felt his wet finger prod her back hole. She jerked, which made her moan as it pushed her clit into him.

She opened her eyes wide to find him watching her closely as he slowly teased that other entrance.

"They say that there are a lot of nerve endings here," he said. "I've always wanted to give a woman this pleasure, but it's never been right. If it hurts, just tell me and I'll stop."

She swallowed hard then nodded. He bent his head back to her clit, giving it one long swipe. His other hand began fucking into her pussy, his tongue assaulting her clit as that one finger slowly pushed its way in.

Hillary screamed at the pleasure and began coming as he moved the finger in and out. He let go of her clit and replaced his hand in her pussy with his cock, fighting his way in, causing her orgasm to ratchet up to a whole new level. He pulled his finger from her ass and pounded into her. It only took a few strokes before she came again, triggering his own release. He collapsed beside her.

"Holy hell," she said.

"Yeah," he agreed.

"How are we going to get to the bed?"

He seemed to think about that for a minute. "Do we *need* to get to the bed?"

She considered this. "I think we'll get cold without the blanket."

She barely managed to roll her head to look at him.

He rolled his head the other way to look at the bed. "Huh." He grunted. Neither of them moved.

After about an hour, or possibly five minutes, Zachary groaned as he reached the hand closest to the bed out and managed to grasp a handful of the spread. He gave a mighty heave and pulled it to them. Hillary roused enough to snuggle into him underneath it.

CHAPTER SEVEN

I n the morning Hillary had a decision to make. She could stay there another day with Zach, then go to work the following week, allowing him to deal with her past, keeping her informed by phone. Or she could gather up her courage and go with him today, meet the pack, and work with him on whatever needed to be done. After that she could go to work, but then she'd feel comfortable, in theory at least, returning to him, and the pack, when and if the need should arise.

There was really no decision, of course. Once she acknowledged the fact that meeting the pack still scared her, despite Zach's assurances and love, there was nothing for her to do but face it head on. She wouldn't allow her fears, based on what those bastards had done to her, to rule her life any longer. She was past that now and besides, with Zach by her side, surely there was nothing she couldn't do.

Hillary watched Zach at the stove as she sat on the kitchen counter. He was wearing jeans but nothing else. She'd never seen anything sexier than this man, cooking her breakfast, his chest bare. He was so casual, so relaxed, so sure of himself. When she stopped to think about it, she was still shocked by how quickly her feelings for him had become so powerful. There was no denying it though—she felt the love in every part of herself, down to the bone.

"So," she began, as he transferred the eggs to a plate. "We should go to your house today, don't you think? It'll be easier to do everything we need to do. Call people, make plans, whatever. You can introduce me to the rest of your family, and the pack if you're ready." She tried to sound relaxed, wasn't sure she succeeded.

Zach was buttering the toast. He didn't look at her, didn't answer her for a moment. He cut the toast into triangles then wiped his hands on a towel. Finally he turned to her, searching her face carefully. He stepped up to the counter where she sat, nudging her knees apart so that he could step between them.

"There's nothing wrong with taking this day for just the two of us, as we'd planned. We're mated, we both know that and feel that, sure. That doesn't mean we shouldn't take the time for ourselves to actually get to know each other." He let his hands rest on her waist, his thumbs brushing idly over her stomach. "Then there's the fact that nobody's here to distract us from anything else we might like to explore." He leaned in, nipped her chin.

"Are you saying that we wouldn't be able to do those things at your house?" she asked, her words not coming out quite as steadily as she would have liked as his hands inched higher. She moaned as he stepped back, taking her hand in his to help her hop off the counter.

"Eggs are getting cold. You are so going to need your energy," he said with an exaggerated leer.

"The truth is, I love being here alone with you. Yes, we can be alone at my house, but there's a price to pay to being the alphas. There'll be interruptions, and everyone will be wanting to meet you."

They sat down at the table and she took a bite of eggs while he continued.

"I very much want to introduce you to the pack, because they need you and because you'll see that they're not only not scary to a

badass werewolf like yourself, but that they're here for you." He took a bite of his breakfast while she thought about that.

"I want you to see, to feel, the support that they're going to give to you, first off because you're my mate and their alpha, but then because you're you and they won't be able to help loving you. But there's also the part of me that wants to keep you to myself, right here, alone, forever."

She leaned over their plates and kissed him, long and hard. When she was done, she pulled back then darted back in to get a crumb from the corner of his mouth. "Let's get this whole Arizona crap taken care of, then you and I can take a vacation together. We can do that, right?"

He smiled, finishing off his eggs and toast. "I like that plan. Yes, that's what the hierarchy is for, so that everything doesn't have to be on our heads all of the time. Luckily, we have a very good hierarchy."

"Good," she said, picking up their plates. "Then let's go meet them."

They talked in Zach's SUV, learning more about each other. They had a lot in common, opinions about books, politics and religion, as well as some differences that made for good, spirited debates, especially over music. As they approached Mountain View though, Hillary became quiet.

Zachary reached over to take her hand, bringing it to his lips once for a kiss. "When we get home, I'll call the hierarchy, have them come over first. They can get the word out that you're here and plan a pack meeting for tonight. We'll give them a quick rundown, so they know what's going on."

Hillary nodded, squeezed his hand. She was watching the scenery, so similar to her little town of Slade. As they drove through the town, she tried to see what businesses there were. He glanced over at her then grinned. "Are you sure you don't want to tell me what kind of shop you have?"

She looked at him, worried he might be upset she was keeping something so basic a secret from him, but he was obviously teasing her. "Why don't you guess?" she asked, raising an eyebrow at him in challenge.

He barked out a laugh. "Right, I'm not that stupid. That's a trap guaranteed to get me into trouble somehow. I'll just wait, with bated breath I might add, for you to discuss your secret with my brother." He grinned again, showing her it wasn't something he was worried about, then grew serious. "I just want to make sure you'll be happy here, Larry, doing whatever you want to do. In fact, you don't really even have to work, if you don't want to."

She gave him a look. "Right, I can just see myself now, waiting for you at the door when you come home, apron on, martini in hand."

He stuck his tongue out and panted like a dog. "Sounds great to me. But that's not exactly what I meant. You'll find that being alpha can be a full-time job, if you want it to be, or let it be. Sort of like being a full-time parent. Speaking of which..."

He squeezed her hand again. Hillary swallowed, then said, "I'm not really ready to think about that yet, Zach. I know that I'd love to have children with you someday, if that's what you want. But not for a while. Which sounds pretty stupid considering I haven't once asked you to wear a condom."

Zach kissed her hand again then freed it as he pulled off the highway. "While the thought of you pregnant with our child is seriously turning me on, there's certainly no rush. I swear that I'm totally disease-free, which the pack doctor can confirm. As far as pregnancy, I'll know when you're in heat and we can do the condom thing then."

"In *heat*?" Hillary spluttered, but Zach just laughed.

"Maybe you should talk to Tracy about that part," he suggested.

They drove another twenty minutes before he pulled off onto a road marked "private property". They went a couple of miles and reached a security gate. Zach stretched out the window to punch in a code. "I'll get Alex to get you all of the keys and codes that you'll need. He handles security. It's hard to keep the woods secure, since it needs to be open to our running around, but we do our best to keep the house itself closed and monitored. There hasn't ever really been a threat, but we want to be prepared. Plus, wolves don't deal well with human burglars, so it's best to keep them discouraged from trying." As he spoke they rounded a bend and Hillary saw a gorgeous two-story house, at least five thousand square feet. She looked at him in astonishment.

He smiled sheepishly. "My family has always been well off. The family business is paper, and, well, as much as people thought computers would be the end of paper, it's really not going to happen."

She rolled her eyes at him and looked back at the house. "It's beautiful."

"I'm glad you like it, but if you want something else, it's not a problem. I bought this when it came on the market because it was the closest neighbor to the pack acreage. It pretty much doubled what we can call ours. Someone else from the pack would certainly be willing to take it over."

They got out of the SUV and headed inside. If she'd had time to think about it, Hillary would have worried that the large, gorgeous house would be too formal inside for her, too rich, too stuffy. When they stepped inside however, she knew immediately that she could feel at home here. The décor was warm and comfortable, the furniture inviting, though well-appointed. She wondered if Zachary had used a decorator, as every room was clearly put together, but not with the stuffy feeling she expected from an interior designer.

Zachary was watching her, judging her reaction, and it finally dawned on her that he was worried she wouldn't like the place. She believed him when he said that if she wanted to find another house, he would do so without hesitation, but it was also clear that he liked this house. She smiled at him, "I really like it, Zach. I like it a lot. Who decorated it?"

PLEASED THAT HILLARY liked his house, Zach relaxed. He hadn't actually realized how worried he was about that until she'd given her approval. He'd meant what he'd said, of course. If she wanted to move, they would move. But he liked this house and the land. "My sister Molly's best friend is a decorator. The two of them did everything. I made very few changes once I moved in." He hugged her to him tightly. "I want you to be completely comfortable, Larry, so if there's anything you want to change, it's all yours." He kissed her then grabbed her hand and pulled her about to show her the rest of the impressive home.

There was a comfortable family room done in browns and blues. A large-screen television hung from one wall and a built-in bookshelf covered the rest. Hillary walked to the books to check out his selections, but he decided that he wanted to see what his couch looked like with her draped over it. A gentle side-check landed her on the soft leather. He'd been right, she was the perfect accessory. His hands went naturally to her hips, one of his favorite things to hold on to, he'd discovered.

"Zach," she laughed at him. "We're supposed to be touring the house. People will be here soon." But she didn't stop his hands as they moved up her sides, taking the t- shirt with them. Her smooth skin called to him and he lowered his head to make designs with his tongue. When her breathing became ragged he forced himself up, holding out a hand to her.

"Sorry, baby, I couldn't resist seeing how much better the couch looks with you on it. We'd better get moving."

She gave him a look that was stuck between hot and disgusted. He managed not to laugh. He was going to have fun teasing her. If he could hold out. The problem with teasing Hillary was that it enticed him just as much as it did her. Taking his hand, she let him pull her up off the couch.

He brought her into the kitchen, one of his favorite rooms in the house.

"Let's see what the bachelor alpha has in his refrigerator." She flashed him a grin and opened the stainless steel door.

He may be a bachelor but he had frequent visitors of the hungry werewolf type, so the fridge was stocked full. Crowding in behind her, he let his heat blanket her back while the cold air assaulted her from the front. She shivered against him. Though he didn't go under her shirt this time, he brought his hands up to her breasts. As he'd hoped, her nipples had begun to peak. He pinched at them through the cloth of her shirt and bra, pulling them out. She gave a low moan and dropped her head to rest against him. For counterpoint, he placed a hot, wet kiss on her neck. Then he stepped back, careful to support her until she was steady on her feet. She turned to glare at him.

"Baby, there are a lot more rooms in this house. We'll never make it through if you keep distracting me."

He grabbed her hand and turned before she could see the grin he couldn't hold back. Leading her into the dining room, he let go of her hand and braced both of his on the walnut table, putting his weight into it. He looked over his shoulder at her.

"I never really tested how steady this was before, but I think it'll do." He gave her a deliberate once-over to make sure she knew exactly what he was thinking.

She rolled her eyes but didn't get close enough for him to touch her. Plus, she was fighting a smile, he was sure.

Rather than continue through the house, he decided to take a small detour to the back deck. The backyard sloped down to the woods so the deck ended up being about five feet off the ground. It ran the length of the house and was perfect for watching the sun set on a warm evening. The railing was wide and sturdy so he turned and hopped up onto it, pulling Hillary between his open legs.

"What do you think of the view?" he asked.

She stared right at him. "It'll do." Then she kissed him. He would never get enough of kissing this woman.

A smug look flicked over her face but he pretended not to notice that he'd seen the moment she decided to turn the tables on him. She stepped in just a little bit closer, letting her head rest against his shoulder, but also letting her tightened nipples poke into his shirt.

She took deep breaths, letting the tips draw along his chest. A dangerous game, as he knew, since she would be getting just as turned-on as he was.

"Tired, Larry? Maybe we should take a nap."

"Mmm. Later. You still have to show me the rest of the house." But she didn't move away. Her hands slid around his waist to cup his ass above the railing.

She gave a squeeze and his cock jerked in response. He felt her smile into his neck. Getting bolder and bolder every hour, and he loved it. Pushing her back gently, he hopped down. "All right then, let's see the rest."

He led her to the door that opened into his study. It had a desk and more bookshelves, but no couch, as he would be too tempted to nap. "We could put another desk in here, there's space. Or there's a different room I'll show you that you might consider." The idea of working in there together was appealing, but he wondered how much work he might actually get done.

Copying him, Hillary walked to his desk and tested its sturdiness. Then she turned and boosted herself up, sitting on the cherry wood, feet dangling, giving him an innocent look. Yeah, probably wouldn't get much work done at all. He walked to her, setting his hands on her knees, pushing her legs apart as he slid his hands up her thighs.

"Are you wet for me?" he murmured, his mouth an inch from hers, his hands at the tops of her thighs.

"Y-yes."

"Mmm. Can I see?"

"Sure." Her breathy sigh belied her cocky answer.

He slid this thumbs to the seam of her jeans, pressing hard against her as he drew them up then moved to the closure. She leaned back on her hands, giving him access to the button and zipper, which he released quickly. He brought one hand up to cup her neck and bring her in for a kiss while he slid the other inside her jeans and cupped her very wet panty-covered mound. He kept his hand still while he explored her mouth with his, once again

learning the shape and taste of her. This time it was his own ragged breathing that reminded him it was time to move on.

"We should, uh..." he swallowed, tried again. "We should get on with the tour." She narrowed her eyes at him. Then she laughed.

"What?"

"Well, you'd need to move your hand before we could do that."

He looked down. Sure enough, his hand was still inside her jeans, gently massaging her. He met her eyes and they both laughed. Pulling free, he helped her down and zipped her up. The chances of making it through the whole house weren't looking so great. He at least had to get her upstairs.

Out of the study he pulled her down the hall, moving at a much brisker pace. "Here's a spare bedroom we could make into an office for you, if you like."

She gave it a brief glance but didn't seem any more interested in looking it over than he did.

"Okay."

"Okay. Great." He moved down the hall. "Laundry room, door to the garage, we can check that out later, another door to the patio, game room. Do you like to play pool?"

"Uh-huh, sure. It's nice, can't wait to explore it. Later." She barely looked through the doorway.

They arrived back at the front hall. He waved in the direction they hadn't taken. "Formal living room."

She didn't even look, just headed for the stairs. "Got it. Living room. Bedrooms up here?"

"Yep." Her butt was at eye level and it was more temptation than he could stand. He cupped the cheeks, satisfied to watch a shiver race up her spine. When she got to the top of the stairs he let her go. She took two steps into the hallway and turned to face him. All teasing was over, he knew it and she knew it. And they weren't going to make it to the bed, damn it.

He moved in, taking her mouth in as sweet and gentle a kiss as he could manage while returning his hands to her glorious rear. She gripped his hair, holding him close. He breathed her in. Ah hell. He slammed her against the wall, the kiss going from sweet to combustible in a nanosecond. More, he needed more. He scrambled to undo her jeans. Why the hell had he rebuttoned them? He finally managed it and pushed them down, without breaking the kiss. While she kicked her pants away, he attacked his own, stripping them off in record time. He lifted her up and her legs immediately wrapped around his waist. Who needed a bed?

Her hands released their tight grip on his hair and she tore her mouth free of his just as he surged into her. She screamed. Oh, how he loved making her scream. He leaned in and licked her neck, tasting salty sweat and sweet, sweet Hillary. Her legs tightened around him and she squeezed him tight.

"Oh fuck, baby." He knew he sounded desperate, and he was. But she was right there with him. She tore his shirt open and ran her fingers along his chest and over his shoulders. Her fingers raked his back with a delicious sting. "Take your top off. Now."

She tweaked his nipple instead, pulling on it.

"Hillary. Shirt. Now."

This time she complied and the minute the fabric was above her breasts he was there, not even waiting to deal with her bra. He sucked her nipple into his mouth while it was still covered in lace.

Her head fell back. "Zach. Please."

He bit down and her whole body shattered in his arms.

Releasing her nipple, he buried his head in her shoulder and pumped into her one more time before coming so hard he worried for just an instant that he might drop her.

She dropped her legs down and he leaned back so he could see her face. Her smile was deeply satisfied. "So. Are there any bedrooms up here?"

He grinned. "One or two. Would you like to see ours?"

"Yeah. That would be nice."

He picked up their discarded clothes while she removed her bra. They didn't even pretend to look at the rest of the floor as he led her to the master bedroom at the end of the hall. Waving vaguely at the room he went straight to the bathroom and turned on the shower. Hillary peeled his shirt off him and they stepped in.

He nuzzled her neck while she washed his hair. "I'm sorry we have to hurry. I should have scheduled things better."

"Neither of us is used to scheduling time for lots of sex, I guess," she laughed. Then her fingers paused their massaging motion and she looked at him, eyes wide.

He smiled. "I won't claim to have been a monk, but there were few scheduling conflicts when it came to time for sex. Unlike now." He grabbed the bottle of shampoo and returned the favor. Worried that they may have already run out of time, he concentrated on the wolves of the hierarchy. Shit, yes, they were coming closer. Hillary blinked up at him, having felt a little bit of that connection. Then she realized what it meant and picked up her pace.

They dried off quickly and were just moving back down the hall with the idea of continuing the tour when a loud beep interrupted them. He showed her the security panel on the wall.

"I'll show you how all of this works when you feel like learning some technical stuff. Or, if you prefer to learn directly from the master, Alex can show you." He pushed some buttons and looked at a small screen. "That's Alex's car, and it looks like he has Molly and Travis with him too."

As they reached the bottom stair, Zachary came to an abrupt halt. "Shit. We didn't talk about the way they'll behave, greeting their new alpha. If you think you might be uncomfortable with it for now, you can go upstairs and I'll explain it to them. They all understand that people raised human need to come into this gradually."

HILLARY BREATHED IN DEEPLY, seeing the absolute trust and love in her man's eyes. "I read about some of it on the website. I'll just go with the flow. I'll look at you if I'm not sure about something, and if you find it all normal, I won't worry about it." She wrapped her arms around his neck, meeting his lips with hers. "I love you, Zachary Jenner," she whispered, meaning it down to her toes.

He closed his eyes in pleasure then opened them to show her his love. "I love you, Larry Abbott."

"I can't believe you like that ridiculous nickname. Todd will just love that about you." They walked to the door and opened it, waiting on the threshold, arm in arm.

Molly was older than her brothers, her blonde hair cut in a sassy bob, her face showing excitement with a little bit of nerves, her green eyes sparkling. Her husband Travis was the same height as she, dark hair, with a wiry body that he moved with a subtle grace, giving Hillary an impression more of a panther than a wolf. They both stopped on the walkway, slightly below Zachary and Hillary. They lowered their heads a little in submission, breathing deeply, clearly testing her scent and power. Their heads lowered another fraction, in unison, and Hillary could actually feel the moment that they accepted her position above them.

She couldn't keep from glancing at Zach, a little wide-eyed. Being prepared not to act foolishly despite any strange actions the wolves made toward her wasn't the same as knowing how she was supposed to act toward them. Zachary raised the hand not holding hers up to his sister, who was directly in front of him. Hillary mimicked him with her free hand, touching Travis' shoulder.

She gave a small gasp, unable to contain the surprise she felt when she touched the wolf. She could distantly feel the connection Zach made with his sister. She closed her eyes, concentrating on the sensation, feeling it zip through her. It felt as if she was making a place for them inside her, mapping their location inside her heart, her soul.

She released Zach's hand and raised her other hand to Molly, feeling that connection strengthen to the same power as Travis'.

Her hands tightening their grip on their shoulders, her mouth open and her eyes still closed, Hillary breathed in, letting the sensations settle inside her, feeling their power from inside her body. It was the oddest feeling, but not unpleasant. She felt as if she couldn't wait to get to know these people, her wolves. She opened her eyes self- consciously, not sure how much time had passed while she had stood there with her eyes closed, expecting to find everyone staring at her. Molly and Travis, however, had tilted their heads, baring their throats to her, their eyes closed now too. She moved her hands from their shoulders, cupping the backs of their necks, and smiled.

Everyone dropped their hands as Zach, smiling hugely now that the formal pack introduction was made, introduced his wife to his sister and her mate. "Larry, this brat is my favorite sister, Molly, and her very patient husband, Travis. Molly, Travis, this is my mate, Hillary."

Moving slowly, clearly prepared to be rebuffed, but willing to take the chance, Molly leaned in front of her husband and gave Hillary a tight hug. Hillary returned the embrace. She could easily feel Molly's pleasure at seeing her brother so happy. Zach stepped back, waving Molly and Travis inside so that he and Hillary could greet Alex, who had been waiting patiently behind the couple.

Alex had bright green eyes and very dark hair with curls that Hillary was sure he hated. He was a little bit taller than Zach, putting him at about eye level from where he stood, which had him a head taller than Hillary. He breathed deeply as he took a couple of steps forward, his eyes bouncing back and forth between Zach and Hillary, then dropped smoothly to his knees in front of Hillary, his head lowered. She reached her hand out and rested it on his head, unable to resist the urge to push her fingers through the curls.

She was ready for it this time, but the feeling was still incredible. The sensation of his soul, his being, bonding with her, not so unlike the bond she'd felt with Zachary when they mated, though on a totally different level, nearly brought tears to her eyes. She could feel his sweetness, his dedication to his pack, his longing to find a mate of his own. She could actually feel the fierce loyalty inside him expanding just enough to add her in, to include her in those people he would cherish and protect with his life.

Leaning down, Hillary kissed his head, urging him to his feet, wondering why she'd felt this more strongly with him than with

Molly and Travis. She looked at Zachary, who was putting out his own hand to help his second stand, and knew that he understood and would explain later.

"Hillary, this is our second, Alex. He is the genius behind our security system. Any help you need with security, or computers or electronics in general, he's your wolf. Alex, this is Larry, my holy-hell-can-you-even-believe-it mate."

Hillary blushed, and the men laughed.

Alex bowed his head again briefly before speaking. "It is my honor to meet you, Alpha, and my pleasure to welcome you, Hillary, to our pack. I can't understand how he could have done it, drugs, maybe, but I am very happy that he did. Can I really call you Larry?" He grinned at her, making his already handsome face even more so, and she hoped she would be able to greet his mate soon, see this man as happy as she and Zach were.

They all walked into the house, going to the family-style kitchen where Molly and Travis waited for them. Hillary could see that they were used to making themselves at home here and had held back for her benefit. She was glad to see that they were making an effort to respect her domain, but knew that she wouldn't be comfortable until they were acting like themselves.

"I want to thank you all for coming here to welcome me. I know I'm supposed to do some kind of fancy wolf thing tonight, but I really appreciate your coming to let me do this privately and in stages."

She looked at Molly. "I know that you guys are a close family, regardless of the pack, and I can't tell you how much I'm looking forward to being a part of that. I didn't have much family growing up and I have none now, so it'll be a lot of fun becoming part of yours. But if I do or say anything that makes you uncomfortable, it's probably just because I'm not used to this, so feel free to talk to me about it."

She sat at on a barstool at the center island next to Travis and waved her hand toward the kitchen. "Since I've only seen the kitchen, not actually tried to find anything in it, you guys are going to have to fend for yourselves, I'm afraid." She put her chin in her hand and glanced at Molly, hoping the woman would catch her meaning and not think she was trying to order them about.

Molly laughed and hugged Zach. "You always did manage to find the best of everything. I don't know why I worried you would do any differently with a mate." She went to sit on Travis' other side. "I'll have an iced tea, please, Alex." She winked at Hillary .

Alex stuck his tongue out at her then went to the fridge, Zachary going to the cupboard next to it to get cups and glasses.

"You thirsty, baby?" he asked Hillary.

"Sure, whatcha got?"

Alex began calling options out, his head in the fridge. The doorbell rang and Hillary gave her drink choice to Alex as she and Zach walked back to the door. He brought her to a halt before they reached it, giving her a kiss.

"Okay so far?" he asked.

She smiled up at him, "You were right, the anticipation is what's scary, but it all feels so natural once I actually meet them."

They continued on toward the door.

"You'll find the link with the unmated wolves a little bit more intense than with the mated wolves," Zach said, answering her unspoken question from when they'd greeted Alex. "It's natural, part of what will help you know when they find their own mate. Also, when they have mates, they aren't as dependent on the pack, on us, for direct support, since they have that from each other."

She nodded, having realized this to some extent as she examined the bonds that were forming inside her. "Will I really be able to differentiate all of these bonds? Just how many wolves are in our pack again?"

Zach squeezed her shoulder tightly. "It's not something you have to worry about, it just happens. When you think about or talk to one of the wolves, that connection inside you will make itself known, sort of stand out from the others for the time being." He put his hand on the doorknob but didn't turn it. "Think about it. Right now you're thinking of Molly, Travis and Alex, but in the background you have the connections with Aaron and Tracy. Not as strongly, since we weren't mated last time you saw them, but the connection is there. Now that you're thinking about them, and once I open the door, that connection will...I don't know, brighten, I guess."

She nodded her understanding and he opened the door.

Hillary could see Aaron and Tracy, and gave them a brief smile, but her attention was on the wolf in front of her. This had to be Zach's cousin, Peter, the other single wolf of the hierarchy. He was blond, like Molly, his hair long, brushing his shoulders. He was average height, a little shorter than Zach, a little taller than Hillary. He regarded her for a longer moment than the others had, more of a challenge in his perusal of her. Just as Zach began to tense at her side, he went to his knees, carefully placed so that he was centered between Zach and Hillary. Hillary heard a low growl and realized with some astonishment that it was coming from her. Her brain was telling her that nothing strange had occurred, but her instincts, and her wolf, were feeling insulted and challenged.

She examined the feelings inside carefully, more curious than angry, making no move to touch the wolf. She breathed deeply, wanting to make sure what her senses were telling her. Peter had been irritated and...condescending, she thought, when he'd first stood there looking at her, but now he was growing uneasy and, she smiled to herself as she identified the feeling, contrite.

Whatever his problem was it was based on what he'd thought before meeting her and was rapidly being revised now that he could feel her power. She waited another minute and watched with some satisfaction as his back bent further. She reached her hand out to his cheek, stopping him from going lower. He rested his face in her hand, allowing her to support his head. He gave a small whine in apology.

Hillary used her hand on his cheek to raise Peter up, but he kept his gaze down, even as he stood before her. She moved her hand down his neck to rest against his heart, and focused herself on what was happening inside. As with the others, she felt the connection being created. She was able to judge his power in comparison with the rest of the hierarchy, could see how they each differed enough to warrant their ranks.

When she felt that the connection had solidified, she gently pushed on Peter's shoulder so that he would bend down enough for her to place a kiss on his forehead. She felt his whole body relax, only then realizing how tense he'd become since first standing before them.

Zach put his hand on Peter's arm and guided him inside the house, not saying a word to him. Hillary turned back to Aaron and Tracy and moved forward to hug them before they could move into wolf mode. She was glad to see them. She couldn't imagine how much more difficult meeting the new wolves would have been if it hadn't been for Aaron and Tracy's easy and immediate acceptance of her. She laughed as Aaron took her from Tracy in a bear hug, lifting her all the way off the ground. She put her nose into his neck, inhaling deeply, finding contentment in the knowledge that this man was her friend and that he would protect and support her in any way she might ask. "Thank you," she whispered into his ear.

Zachary cleared his throat, although when Hillary turned back to him he was clearly fighting to keep a grin from his face. She returned to his side, gently elbowing him in the ribs. Aaron and Tracy bowed their heads. Hillary reached a hand to each of them, laughing as she felt the bond that already existed flare brighter. It was obvious to her that the bond with these two would always cut a little bit deeper than it would for the rest of the pack. They were the first that she truly had felt were hers, and she would take care of them and cherish them—her friends.

They all went inside, reconvening in the kitchen.

"Whew," Hillary said, putting a hand on her stomach. "I think I could eat now."

Everyone laughed, and worked together as a group to put sand-wich makings on the island, along with plates and whatever else they decided might be good for lunch. At last everyone was seated, with food and drink.

Molly cleared her throat and began. "Congratulations, both of you. Zach, we're thrilled you found someone so special at last, and Hillary, we are truly pleased to welcome you into this pack. We've been waiting a couple of years for Zachary to find his mate and make this pack truly complete, and it doesn't take more than a minute in your presence to know that you'll be good for him, as well as the rest of us."

Everyone else nodded and beamed their agreement while Hillary blushed.

Zach leaned over and kissed her cheek. He gestured to the group. "Everyone here will be more than happy to answer any questions you have about the pack or werewolves in general. Later, when we meet the rest of the pack, I'm going to introduce you to my friend Taylor and his mate Claire. Taylor was human, so he'll have a better sense of what you're going through as far as introduction to werewolf life in general." He looked back to the group, and Hillary could feel him pulling on his alpha mantle, saw the hierarchy react, become serious.

"Hillary wasn't converted by our mating. She was converted four years ago by attack." He paused briefly, feeling the swell of aggression in the room, letting it settle somewhat before he continued. "We've figured out that the group appears to be based around a family outside Phoenix, Arizona, led by a man named Ken Cage. Cage and his brother's family, John, Shannon and son Jeff, are the only Cages listed on the membership list for the Mesa Pack. The pack roster shows them still living in Tucson, where the pack is based. Do any of you know anything about Mesa?"

Travis frowned. "My sister mated into the Colorado Pack, lives in Denver. Her pack is kind of small and she mentioned once that it was a shame that the closest pack was Mesa, that they were a pretty weak pack, so Colorado doesn't make much effort to interact with them."

He stood up, moving around the table to slide his hand along Hillary's back as he went to the fridge, even though that was taking the long way around the table. She felt the comfort of his touch and knew that what she'd read on the website was true. Touch was used by the wolves as comfort. Young wolves had to be lectured on being careful around their human counterparts, that touch meant different things to humans than to werewolves.

Alex spoke up. "National Council hasn't had any reports of unusual activity, at least since I've been a member these last two years. The closest rep to that area, that I can think of, is Texas. Sara Todd is their second. I can talk to her, see what she thinks of the alphas. It would be her responsibility to talk to them occasionally, at least once a year, see if they had any concerns they need her to address to the council."

Alex thought a moment. "Travis is right, they're a small pack. They don't, collectively, have a lot of power. I guess, if I think about it like that, it's not too much of a stretch to imagine that this Cage guy could be building his own pack without the alphas' knowledge." He looked at Zach. "Is that what you're thinking?"

Zachary nodded. "Yes, at the time there were probably about twenty or so wolves." He glanced at Hillary who nodded her confirmation. "In addition to finding this so- called pack and shutting it down permanently, we need to find out if there were any other..." Hillary gripped his hand as his sentence turned into a growl, ratcheting up the tension of all the wolves there. "Escapes. If someone is out there who needs our help." Hillary swallowed hard.

"How likely is it, if someone was successfully turned from the attack, that they would just go along with it, join the pack? Would the...loyalty, the urge to support the pack, would that still be there in that kind of situation?" Her brows furrowed, the idea causing her stomach to knot.

"I've been thinking about this since we met," Aaron said. "One of the reasons that planned attacks, with the intent of converting, as opposed to attacks of aggression that are spur of the moment, are so unusual, is that a person has to be really strong to survive the attack and convert. There aren't really statistics on it, because it's so rare, but I would say very few humans survive. Which means that those who do," he bowed his head respectfully to Hillary, "turn into *very* strong wolves."

Everyone at the table, except for Hillary, smiled with fierce pride. She casually took a long drink from her glass, while Zachary chuckled.

"The point is," Aaron continued. "If you think it would be a great idea to add to your pack numbers this way, you'd have to be pretty stupid, because the chances are good that the new wolf would be too powerful to just meekly accept a position in the pack."

"But if this is all so rare, like you guys are saying, they might not realize all of that."

Zachary nodded, "So the question is, did Cage really expect anyone to survive, or was he just using it as a handy excuse to rape and murder a beautiful woman?"

Hillary found herself in the unexpected position of comforting the seven wolves around her, who were getting more and more upset. She sent calming thoughts along their bonds and used her hand to turn Zach's face to her. His jaw was clenched, but she kissed him anyway, until he finally softened, relaxing into the kiss, claiming her mouth with a deep sigh before letting her pull away.

Aaron had his arm around Tracy, and Molly was rubbing her hand along Travis' back, while he nibbled on her other hand. Alex and Peter had come to stand behind Zach and Hillary and when she glanced back at them they moved in, laying hands on their backs and shoulders. She could feel them relaxing, allowing themselves to be soothed by their alphas. Suddenly, she was so tired, all of the emotions she'd been sensing, feeling and sharing had drained her, plus her sleep had been somewhat interrupted last night, she thought with a grin. She leaned her head on Zach's shoulder, which Alex had been resting his hand on. Alex moved his hand to her head, stroking it lightly .

Zachary looked at his watch. "Dinner with the pack is scheduled for seven. Let's meet at the pack house at six thirty. In the meantime, Alex, will you contact the National Secretary, let him know what's going on? I think you should hold off on the Texas rep until

we see what the secretary says. Travis, go ahead and call your sister and her mate. Tell them we have a young wolf who's thinking of moving to Mesa and you just want to get a general idea of what the pack is like."

They all rose, saying their goodbyes. As soon as the door shut behind them, Zachary swept Hillary up into his arms and bounced up the stairs to his bedroom. He undressed her, pulled the covers back and gently helped her into bed. He took off his own clothes and got in, holding her tightly to him. She was asleep in minutes.

CHAPTER EIGHT

W hen Hillary woke up she was on her stomach, her head lying on Zach's chest. He had one hand resting on her back but she gently squirmed out from under it, deciding this was her chance. She sat up and waited to see if he was going to stay asleep. After a moment, when his breathing remained even, she smiled. Gently, she eased back the sheet, pushing it down to his knees.

She swallowed hard as she looked at the gorgeous man spread out before her. She licked her lips, her eyes devouring the tight body. There was so much she wanted to touch! She decided today was not the day to tease herself, or him, and went straight for the gold. She scooted her body down and sat at his hip, legs crossed in front of her. She studied his cock. *Her cock*, she thought with another big grin. She leaned over to get a better look. Even at rest, it was larger than she would have expected. Her warm breath caressed it, causing it to twitch. Hillary gave a small hum of pleasure. She experimented, giving it another warm breath then pursing her lips to blow a cool stream. There was definite movement.

Reaching out her hand, Hillary gently picked it up, marveling at the texture, amazed to feel it stretch and lengthen in her palm. She squeezed gently and it jerked. Licking her lips again, she leaned down and gently touched the very tip of her tongue to the tip of Zach's penis. Distantly she was aware that his breathing had become erratic. As the cock in her hands lengthened, she kept her palm tight around the shaft and took it into her mouth. Her lips closed around the head and she sucked in hard. She breathed deeply, loving the smell of him, the taste of him, the feel of him. She cut her eyes up to Zach's face, found him watching her, sweat beaded on his forehead. She used her tongue to see what else she could feel, working it around the head, flicking it, watching his reaction.

"Fuck, baby, I'm not going to be able to stand it if you do that much longer."

Hillary merely raised her eyebrow at him, using one hand to trace his balls.

"Aargh," was all he managed before he reached up, grabbing her by the waist and swinging her hips toward his head.

Hillary hung on to her prize, determined to do more exploring. She squeaked as Zachary lifted her hips up, landing her stomach to his chest, spreading her legs so that her knees rested on either side of his shoulders. She braced her forearms against him and renewed her concentration as he pulled her pussy to his mouth.

One long swipe of his tongue had Hillary's eyes rolling up in her head. She decided the time for exploring was done and took as much of him into her mouth as she could. He groaned and she spasmed, feeling the vibrations of that groan. Hillary gave a low hum and was pleased to receive a similar reaction. She began to work herself up and down on his shaft, only to be sidetracked by his fingers plunging into her. She raised her head to gasp, giving him the opportunity to roll her to her back and flip around so that his body was pressing her into the mattress. She suppressed a shiver, trying to decide if she should be mad that he'd stopped her. His mouth came down on hers, firm and insistent. She couldn't deny him.

She lost herself in the kiss, the demanding thrust of his tongue mating with hers and his body pressing down on her. Her arms came up to circle him, pull him tighter to her, but he grasped her wrists and pulled them over her head. He broke the kiss, pulled his mouth from her reach and she struggled against his hold, trying to follow him.

"I love you." So simple. So true.

She opened her mouth to respond but was too busy gasping for breath as he suddenly kneeled up, lifted and turned her so that she was facedown before he fell back on top of her. His cock was hard against her inner thigh, his breath heavy in her ear. She waited, unsure of what he was planning now. Rewarding her acquiescence with a nibble on her ear, he slowly lifted up. When she continued to stay still he gave a rumble of pleasure as his hands returned to gripping her wrists. She would have to tease him later about his purring, but for now she was too curious to see what her alpha wolf had planned, to distract him.

He changed his grip so that he held both of her wrists in one hand and was able to slide the other down her back, around her hip and under her belly. Gently he lifted her up until she had her knees under her. His mouth traced wet kisses up her spine until he was stretched over her again, his front warm against her back, his cock hard against her ass, his free hand moving up to cup her breasts and tug on her nipples.

"Zach." It probably should have been a protest but she recognized it for the sound of need that it truly was.

"I'm here, baby." He'd never sounded so guttural, so close to the edge. She kept her smile inside as she determined the best way to send him over the edge. He was driving her crazy, no doubt about it, but there was no reason she had to be there by herself.

Pulling in a deep breath, she set her abs and rotated her ass, keeping the rest of her body perfectly still. There was no holding back the smile this time as he groaned in her ear. He gave her nipple a sharp tug in retaliation. She stopped the rotation and simply tilted her pelvis, driving herself harder onto him.

"Fuck!"

He let go of her wrist, released her breast and slid his hands down her sides until he was kneeling up behind her, a firm grip on her hips. Her body tensed in anticipation. God, she needed him, needed him now.

"Zach, please, now—"

Hard and fast he came into her, hips slamming into her ass, as they both shouted. He pulled back, almost all the way out, fighting against her clenching muscles, then surged back in. So good, it was so good but she needed more.

"Zach." It was barely a whisper this time, but he answered with his body. Draping over her, he came down, kissing the corner of her eye, the corner of her mouth, then tucking his face into her neck and licking her shoulder. She felt the tiniest hint of teeth and somehow went softer around him. This time his growl was nothing like a purr as he resumed fucking her.

Hot steel filled every inch of her, hard warmth surrounded her, and his absolute love for her invaded her every pore. With a soft moan she gave in to the surge of electricity, rode the wave for what felt like hours. When she thought it was almost over, thought she could catch her breath, he pulled her earlobe between his teeth and brought his hand up to pinch her nipple, catapulting her back into the maelstrom. This time he came with her and his seed filling her dragged her under further. Her vision dimmed and her awareness of the world went gray. There was only Zach. Always Zach. Her knees gave out as he pulled free from her, causing a tiny aftershock to roll through her pussy. She let her legs slide out straight and closed her eyes.

Zach rolled to his side next to her and shoved a pillow under their heads. She blinked at him. His smile was a tiny bit smug, but she supposed he deserved it. Still. She summoned the energy to bring her hand up, ran her fingers through his hair, then smacked him lightly on the head.

"Hey!" he protested, without moving.

"I was taking my turn, and you know it!"

"I know, baby. I swear, I tried, I just couldn't do it."

"Hmph."

"I'll make it up to you, Larry, I promise."

He was trying for contrite, but couldn't quite pull the expression off. "You better, tough guy. I would've thought you'd be more practiced at holding out."

"It's you, Larry, there's nothing I can do when it's you."

"Hmph," was all she could say, without her voice betraying her pleasure at his words.

Only the thought of not having time to prepare for meeting the rest of the pack gave her the energy to get out of bed a little while later. They showered, Hillary smacking his hands a number of times while he washed her, Zachary having to grab her hands and hold them away from him more than once while she did the same. Eventually they were dressed and on their way to the pack house.

As they headed out, Hillary was glad to realize that she wasn't really nervous. Well, okay, maybe a little bit, but not as she'd been before meeting the hierarchy. She knew now that what happened would be natural, that there wasn't really anything expected of her that she wouldn't want to give.

"So who lives at the pack house?" she asked.

"Any werewolves who are at loose ends, don't want to live on their own but no longer want to live with their parents. It's where meetings and get-togethers are held, and where the pack congregates at the full moon to run together. The pack has some businesses and some of those funds are earmarked for the house. Any wolf living there has to contribute a certain amount of rent as well as some effort in the house maintenance."

As they pulled up to the house, Hillary could see that a number of people were already there, a few washing their cars, a couple reading on the grass together. She could see some people through the kitchen window, working on dinner.

"Aaron and Tracy, as fourths, are ultimately responsible for the house and it's maintenance but traditionally if the fourth is mated and in their own home, they're allowed to appoint an older member of the pack who's willing to take on the actual duty of living in the house and maintaining order. About five years ago Peter's mother, Sandy, was widowed and she asked if she could take that position."

They got out of the car and walked up to the front door hand in hand. Zachary waved at or called out greetings to everyone they passed, but they continued to the house without being stopped.

"They know we have a meeting before dinner?" Hillary guessed.

"Yes, they don't want to meet you until they're at their best, anyway, so they're happy for us to get inside and let them finish what they're doing so they can go get cleaned up." He led the way to the back of the house and to a door with heavy security.

"This is the office space for the hierarchy, so it's well secured. Not that we've ever had a problem with that kind of thing before, but no sense not being smart about it." He keyed in a code and motioned her through. Peter was already there and he smiled at them as they entered. He bowed to them, more than just a nod of his head.

"All right, Peter, we get it. You're happy Hillary is alpha, Hillary is happy you're third. Who is it exactly that isn't happy?" he asked mildly.

Peter blushed. "Sorry, Alpha, it's my mother. I don't know if you realized how convinced she was that you would be mated to one of her nieces. Remember, she told you they were both coming to visit this summer?"

Zach rolled his eyes. "She'll get over it."

"I know. I was just having a bad day then she called me right after Aaron called about your getting mated and I focused on that instead of what was pissing me off. We do need to talk about that later—it's a problem with the bar." He looked at Hillary. "One of my jobs is managing a bar that we try to keep werewolf only so that the wolves have a place to blow off steam without having to worry too much about the humans."

Hillary nodded as the door opened and Aaron, Tracy, Molly and Travis entered. "Alex was pulling up as we came in the door," Molly said as she put down her purse and took off her jacket. They all greeted each other then Alex as he walked in. When they had taken seats, Zachary began.

"We need to decide if we want to do a formal greeting or casual."

He looked at Hillary and explained. "Usually the formal greeting of a new alpha is when an alpha is taking over, like when I took over from Uncle Sam, or if a new alpha is coming from the hierarchy of a different pack, sort of like a formal transfer from one pack to the other. It's not necessary in this case, since the pack already has an alpha and since you're not leaving a pack behind, giving up your power with them and transferring it to us."

Hillary shrugged her shoulders. "Are there any advantages or disadvantages?"

"Time!" Aaron laughed. "The formal greeting would take a couple of hours as you'd have to lay hands on every wolf, like you did with us this morning. An informal greeting would take about five minutes or so."

"How many wolves are in our pack, and will they all be here?"

Alex answered. "There are one hundred and twenty wolves in Mountain Pack. Everyone will be here tonight except for Chester, who's in South Carolina for the birth of his granddaughter, the four wolves who're currently away at college, one who's on a business trip, and the ten or so who have night jobs and couldn't cancel on such short notice, especially since most of them work for us, so their coworkers are here and can't cover for them.

"With a less powerful alpha I'd be more likely to recommend the formal greeting, to help solidify the bond both ways, but with you there's no doubt that your bond will be strong with every wolf through just the casual greeting. That would normally be the case if the new mate were someone already a part of the pack or who'd grown up visiting frequently."

Hillary furrowed her brow. "How would that happen? Wouldn't they already be mated to the alpha?"

"Sometimes," Tracy answered. "But if two wolves just aren't ready to be mated, the magic doesn't manifest until later. Most often this is when wolves grow up together, and one reaches sexual maturity before the other. My parents were from neighboring packs, so they grew up seeing each other at least a couple of times a year, but it wasn't until my mom visited here when she was a sophomore in college that she and my dad realized they were mates."

"Huh. That makes sense, I suppose. You wouldn't want thirteen-year-olds dealing with the feelings of a mating. So, casual greeting makes sense for everyone?" She looked around, and seeing everyone's nod of agreement, looked to Zachary.

"Let's stick with the greeting for tonight," Zach suggested. "I don't want to bring up the Arizona issue. Everyone will assume Hillary was converted with the mating for now."

Hillary stood up. "I need to speak with Aaron privately for a minute before we go out there." She grabbed his hand and walked to the door, pausing to let him decide where they should go. He led her out into the hall and opened another door.

"We haven't talked about Zach's birthday present. It's driving me crazy not being sure how much I can tell him about my work, which is a big part of who I am. Plus, I have to tell you, I've seen his house and there's nowhere that the table you described to us is going to work there."

"True, but you haven't seen the dining room here yet. Remember, we have to be able to seat up to one hundred and fifty people, sometimes more when other packs come to visit for weddings and whatnot. There's a head table that the hierarchy sit at for formal occasions, as well as visiting hierarchy. Right now it's just a regular table, like all of the others, but I thought it would be cool to do a medieval lord's table."

"All right, I'll check it out when we're in there. In the meantime, I'm going to tell him I own a woodworking shop. I just won't get specific as to the furniture aspect. When is his birthday, anyway?"

"Almost four months," he said with a grimace. "If it gets too awful keeping that much a secret from him, go ahead and tell him I commissioned you to make something for his birthday. He still won't know what it is."

They went back to join the others, who spent the time until dinner telling Hillary more about the pack. When Zach stood, Hillary rose to join him. She took his hand and walked out of the room, surprised at how calm she felt. As they neared the dining room, she began to feel...a sort of humming gathering inside her. She realized that it was the pack she was feeling, a distant connection through Zachary and the rest of the hierarchy.

When they entered the dining room, everyone who wasn't already standing rose to their feet. Zach guided Hillary through the room, bringing her to stand in front of the head table. She allowed him to lead her blindly so that she could focus on the amazing feeling as her soul opened up to receive this pack as hers.

With Zach at her side and the rest of the hierarchy fanned out next to them, Hillary raised her eyes to the pack. Zach spoke, "This is my mate, Hillary Abbott, your new alpha."

As one, the entire group went to their knees. Hillary blinked and looked at Zachary who smiled at her in pride. He squeezed her hand then raised it to his lips to kiss her fingers. She looked back at the pack and said, "Thank you all. I'm so proud to be here, to be yours. Please come and introduce yourselves once you've eaten."

The pack rose to go get their food. Hillary and Zachary went around the table to their chairs while the hierarchy went to the buffet tables to get their food as well. Alex came back to the table with food for all three of them.

"Thanks, Alex," Hillary said. "I didn't think I was hungry, but now that I see this, I'm starved." She smiled at him then looked at her mate and his second.

"Was that normal? Did everything go okay? It felt pretty good, I can feel them all, forming bonds. I can hardly wait to actually start meeting them."

"They didn't have to go to their knees for you," Alex said. "They honored you by doing so. The fact that they all did it at once, without thought, is just another sign of how powerful you are, how powerful you've made Zachary with your bond, and how powerful you've made the pack as a whole, with that bond. We can all feel it, a little something extra that wasn't there yesterday."

She blinked at him. "Wow, okay then. We should eat quickly so that they can come talk to us." She turned to her plate and tried to hide her blush. She could feel the amusement coming from both men, as well as the pride.

As soon as they pushed their plates away, Zach and Hillary turned their chairs so that they could greet any members of the pack who wanted to come meet her personally. They approached singly and in small groups, always polite, never staying long so that others could get their turn. When he introduced her to his friend Taylor, and Taylor's mate Claire, Zach reminded her that Taylor had been human until six years ago. Taylor said that he would be pleased if Hillary came to him with any questions.

When at last it was over, Hillary was exhausted but happy. Some had been very glad to see her, others seemed to be reserving judgment. Hillary couldn't blame them. There was a difference between respecting the power she brought to the pack and reserving judgment on a person's ability to lead well and make important decisions that might affect someone's life.

Most of the pack seemed thrilled to see Zachary happily mated, although more than one had pouted prettily that he was now off the market. A couple of the older ladies gave Hillary a clear appraisal, and she realized that they, like Peter's mother, had harbored hopes for their daughters or nieces. When Peter brought his mother forward to be introduced, she could see that this woman wouldn't be a friend anytime soon, but she was respectful, if not cheerful.

When they got home they collapsed into bed, lying there a moment before helping each other to undress and climb under the covers.

CHAPTER NINE

The next morning Hillary woke to the perfection of Zachary feasting on her pussy. He brought her to the edge, over and over, but pulled back, until she begged him for release. Finally, he reared up, thrusting into her as he looked into her eyes. He pumped once, twice then groaned as her release caused his own.

"I love you," he said, when he could speak. "I'm yours."

Hillary had to swallow around the lump in her throat. "I love you. I'm so glad that you're mine. And so very happy to be yours."

He growled then nipped her shoulder. "Mine," he said fiercely, his teeth still holding on to her. He released her then gently licked the spot.

"Alex will be bringing a couple of guys over this morning," Zachary said as they went into the bathroom to begin their morning. "I assume you still need to get back to your shop today?"

"Yes, and thank you for warning me not to go bounding downstairs naked. I'll need to leave by seven. I'm probably not going to be able to come back until the end of the week. Any chance of your coming down?" She raised her voice since she had stepped into the shower, and Zach was brushing his teeth.

"I need to catch up on things myself, but I'll try to make it down by Wednesday night. There's not much point in my coming down in the day, anyway, since you won't let me in the shop to see my birthday present, right?" he replied after he rinsed his mouth out.

"Figured that out, did you?" She smiled, as they switched places. "Wednesday night will be fine. Just call me when you get near town and I can meet you at the house." She frowned. "I'll need to talk to Todd about renting it. It's not very big, or anything, but it's my first house and I don't want to sell it yet."

"There's no reason you should, if you don't want to. If there's not much of a market for rentals there, we can always use it ourselves as a getaway."

"What's Alex coming by for?" she asked, then waited as he exited the shower and vigorously towel-dried his hair.

"We realized yesterday that you need to have a bodyguard until this thing with Arizona is finished, just in case they get wind of what's going down." He looked hard at her, obviously expecting her to be annoyed, if not angry.

Hillary thought about it for a minute. "You already told me that I'm more powerful than most wolves. If they wanted to kill me, they could just shoot me from a distance, and there's not much a body-guard could do about that. If they attack me with a large group, they'll just make sure the group is large enough to handle two wolves instead of one." Her tone was even and logical. Not arguing, just pointing out the facts and curious to see what his reply would be.

"True, but we do have some wolves who're ex-military and are familiar with security work. Alex actually runs a security company and they work for him, though he usually deals with electronics. They can work to help diminish the danger, advise you on some simple things that can make a difference, like being careful not to be too routine in your movements, making sure your house and shop are secure, that kind of thing. Plus, they'll keep a trained awareness that you wouldn't be able to maintain and shouldn't have to anyway. Lastly, three highly sensitive noses are better than one."

"Plus," Hillary added, "you'll feel better."

"Plus," Zachary agreed, "I'll feel better. It's not that I don't think you can handle yourself, it's that they're trained to think about things like this differently than we are, that's why they're specialists."

"All right," she said, as she breezed past him to get dressed and pack up her things.

He seemed slightly disconcerted about the ease with which she agreed, and Hillary vowed to herself to always try to keep him guessing. She thought it was sweet that he'd take these steps to protect her, to help her protect herself, when there probably wasn't any danger. Besides, just talking about the attack four years ago was making her jumpy. She would be glad to have someone observant around so she wouldn't have to constantly be second-guessing her instincts.

They came down the stairs just as Alex and four other wolves knocked on the front door. Zach went to work the alarm and let them in. They all converged in the kitchen and Hillary and Zachary made breakfast for everyone.

As they ate they chatted about the pack and other non-serious things. Hillary had met the men the previous evening so she knew that one of them was mated with a daughter. She asked about what it was like for a young werewolf to be in school. She assumed that she was supposed to decide which of the men she felt most comfortable with bringing back to stay with her, but she found them all likeable enough. She assumed Alex had already filled them in on the situation and she wouldn't need to explain.

Alex brought the conversation around to their different backgrounds—one had been a police officer in Chicago, two had been marines and one an Army Ranger. Alex quirked a brow at her and she gave him a little shrug, which he correctly read as her opinion that any of the men would do as far as she could decide from this one meeting.

"Okay, here's what I want to do," Alex said, as they cleared the plates. "Hillary, Theo and I will go back with you this morning. If you'll drop me off at your house, you and Theo can go to your office while I check out the home security. Abe will cover for me at work. Anthony will stay here so that when I call in with what I need it can get handled right away. Brad will stay with Zach."

Zach frowned. "Why will Brad stay here?"

Alex looked surprised. "Why wouldn't he? Nobody thinks there's a very real chance of those idiots making a move up here, but if they do, which we need to plan for, there's nearly as big a chance they'll come after you as Hillary. I would plan it as a two-pronged attack myself."

Hillary raised her eyebrow at Zach and he subsided, sheepishly. She nodded at Alex and turned to the men.

"Thank you for doing this. Are you sure you can get away from whatever you were doing?"

Everyone assured her that this was their job and it was easy enough to rearrange things, since the security company was pack owned.

Hillary got into Alex's SUV and began working on a new sketch for Zachary's table. Now that she'd seen the dining room she had some ideas about what she wanted to do with it. She was itching to get her hands on the wood.

They stopped at the cabin and retrieved her car, Theo volunteering to drive it so that she could complete her drawing. She finished it just before they exited the highway and she directed Alex to her home. Part of her was sad that this little house that had seemed so welcoming when she'd moved to Slade would no longer be her home, but she'd gained so much in meeting Zachary that it was nothing in comparison. She reminded herself to tell Todd there would be security upgrades so that he could price the rental accordingly.

Hillary showed Alex and Theo around and invited them to make themselves at home. They left Alex to it and went on to her shop. Theo seemed startled as it had never actually been discussed what her work was. She introduced him to Stephen who eyed the security man appreciatively then grabbed her hand when he noticed her ring. She hugged him and told him that her fiancé's family was connected to a security business and Theo would be checking the security system for the shop and making suggestions on what they should change.

He tried to question her more about her fiancé, but she told him she would explain at lunch. She was eager to finish the mayor's bed so that she could begin work on Zach's table, and he knew her well enough to know that she would focus on that and not want to talk while working.

Confident that with Theo around there was no need for her to be hyperaware, Hillary put her headphones on and chose a hard and fast selection for her work music. As *System of a Down* started up, she let her hands begin their work on the carving for the bedposts.

Hours went by without her notice until Stephen came into her line of sight. He motioned to his watch and she turned off her music. She looked around and saw that Theo had found a position to keep watch from. She dusted herself off and carefully put her tools away.

"All right then, let's eat. Theo, will you call Alex and see if he wants us to pick him up something for lunch? We can take it to the house and eat there. I'm going to call Todd, tell him to meet us there so I don't have to repeat everything twice." She winked at Stephen. "Stephen, will you call the mayor and tell him the bed will be ready for him to come look at tomorrow, if that's convenient?"

They arrived at the house to find Alex waiting for them on the front porch, talking to Todd. Alex smiled at Hillary and then his gaze fastened on Stephen. She heard Stephen gulp as he stood beside her. She tried to keep from smiling in delight, put her arm through Stephen's and brought him up to the door.

"Alex, this is my very good friend and assistant, Stephen. Stee, this is Alex, he's a close friend of my fiancé's. Alex, you've met Todd? Todd, this is Theo." Todd choked at the engagement news and gave her a shocked look. She laughed and pushed them all into the house, Theo bringing the food that they'd picked up.

Stephen had managed to get himself mostly under control by the time they all sat down to eat the burgers and fries. Though his eyes kept flicking to Alex, he was able to keep most of his attention on Hillary as he demanded details.

"Well, Aaron's brother, who we're making the table for? He's, uh, well... He sort of rocked my world, so we're getting married. I just have to figure out the details."

"Jeez," Todd drawled. "When you called and said you had some news, this didn't even make my top ten list of possibilities."

"Sometimes you just know," she said, laughing. She could feel Alex getting more and more tense, and was trying to ignore him.

Todd scrunched his brows. "What's all this got to do with the new security?"

Hillary's face grew serious. "Well, for one thing, the security company is kind of a family business for Zach, so that part is just easy. The other thing is, I have this, um, ex- boyfriend, who, if he hears that I'm engaged, might get a little bit violent. He's kind of crazy. He's the reason I moved to Slade. So keep your eyes open and let me know if you see anything weird."

"Is there any reason that he would hear about your engagement?" Todd asked.

"There is a very distant connection between the Jenners and the ex. That's how I recognized Aaron when he came by the shop last week. Probably he won't even hear about it, but since he's nutso, we figured better safe than sorry for a little while."

"Does this mean you're going to close the shop?" Stephen asked.

"I'm not sure yet. I might move it up closer to Mountain View, I might just open a second shop. There are a few possibilities. I'll definitely want to talk to you about what you think you'd like to do. Maybe you can come visit Mountain View and see if you might want to move there, before we talk about it too much."

She heard a very soft growl from Alex's direction. She bit her cheek to keep from smiling.

"Why don't you come visit this weekend?" She frowned, realizing there might be some issues with that, as far as the wolves were concerned. She looked at Alex. He nodded his agreement. It occurred to her that if the men were mates, and things moved as

quickly for them as it had for her and Zachary, Stephen might already know all about the wolves by the weekend.

That made her remember what Zach had told her about alphas knowing if a human and wolf were mates and her eyes went huge. She looked at Alex but his attention was firmly on Stee. She closed her eyes and concentrated on her connection to him.

"Holy shit," she breathed, feeling the link between the two men come alive. It was as if the connection was glowing, although it wasn't a visible thing. It was an amazing feeling, and she knew that there was no doubt. Very distantly she could feel Zachary become aware of the bond through her.

Beside her, Alex grew even more tense, as if he knew what she'd seen. She opened her eyes and beamed at him, then at Stephen.

"So, um, I need to go with Todd to his office and discuss maybe renting my house out, or something. Theo, why don't you come with us? Stephen, why don't you show Alex the shop for me, so he can do his security thing, then you take the rest of the day off. I'll see you tomorrow."

She jumped up then paused, looking back at Alex. Wasn't she supposed to do something else? Alex nodded at her that her plan was good. She figured if there was more to be done, it could happen later. She grabbed Todd's hand and dragged him out the door, Theo close on their heels.

Hillary glanced at Theo to see if he was aware of what was happening and his grin told her that he was. Todd looked slightly bewildered so she leaned into him and whispered, "I'm trying to set Alex up with Stephen, but you know how much Stephen hates blind dates."

Todd nodded and got in the car. "Do you really want to discuss renting the house? We don't need to go to my office for that. We can go to my house and be more comfortable. That way Maria won't have to grill me for details that I won't be able to give. She can just grill you directly."

"Sounds like a plan to me."

When they got to Todd's, Hillary excused herself to call Zachary.

He answered the phone. "I miss you, baby. I wish I were there."

"I wish you were here too. I wish you could have seen Alex a little while ago when he met Stephen."

"Stephen's your assistant, right?"

"And my friend. He's a good guy. Is there something we're supposed to do?"

"Just help with the coming-out story. The bond was clear enough that I saw it, once you concentrated. Kind of cool, huh?"

"Yeah," she sighed. "That part of the whole werewolf thing is pretty amazing."

"I like it," he said, the smile in his voice obvious. "Will you call me tonight, when you're in bed?" he asked, practically purring.

"Zach! The guys will be down the hall, and their hearing is very good!"

She hung up on his laughter, her smile stretched wide.

CHAPTER TEN

Theo and Hillary returned to her house just as her cell phone rang. She saw that it was Stephen and grinned.

"Hello?"

"Larry." Stephen was whispering.

Hillary resisted the urge to tell him that Alex's hearing was extremely good. "Holy. Fucking. Hell," was all that Stephen managed to say.

"Having a good time, Stee?" she asked.

"I... It's... He." He gulped. "Fuck."

"Sweetie, maybe you could put Alex on the phone for a minute?" There was a fumbling, then the clear sounds of Alex going through the sliding glass door and out into Stephen's backyard.

Alex cleared his throat. "Alpha."

"Everything all right, Alex?" she asked, remembering that this situation wasn't all fun and games.

"It's him."

"Yeah, I kind of gathered that. I thought you already knew?"

"Well yes, sort of, but the reality of it is just so much more than I realized." He took a deep breath. "It's a pretty strong bond, Alpha. I think it will be okay to tell him soon."

"Okay. How about this Wednesday, when Zach gets here? I think he would like to be here for you, when it happens."

"Wednesday. Wednesday works. Alpha, I'm sorry I abandoned my work today. It won't happen again."

"Don't be silly, Alex. If anyone understands what you're going through, I do. At least I didn't have to deal with the whole human thing. I think it will help Stephen when I tell him I'm a wolf, also. As far as your work, why don't you call Anthony tonight with what we need, then he can drive down in the morning. He can be on hand to help Theo with me, so that you're clear to work on the security during the day and spend time with Stee at night."

"Thank you, Alpha."

"You're welcome, Alex. I'm really happy for you. Stephen has been a good friend and I'm so glad that he'll get to remain a part of my life without my having to keep so much a secret from him anymore. Thank you for giving me that."

He laughed. "Believe me, Hillary, the pleasure is all mine."

Hillary wandered into the kitchen, following some amazing smells.

"Theo! You didn't have to cook, but holy cow, that smells good." She leaned over the beef cooking on the stove.

"Well, it is a cow, but I don't think it was holy." He stirred in some more spices. "Beef Stroganoff, my one and only specialty."

"Mmmm. Works for me. Can I help?"

"If you could set the table, I'll be done here in about fifteen minutes. I wasn't sure how many to set up for."

Hillary began setting the table. "I told Alex to stay with Stephen tonight. Anthony will come up in the morning to help out. Are you okay with standing guard on your own tonight?" she asked, pausing to look up at him.

"Sure, we'll be fine. The guestroom is right next to yours, we'll just both leave our doors open."

"I'll call Zachary after dinner, see what news there is from the council."

As they ate the delicious dinner, Theo filled Hillary in on more of the pack history and members. She quizzed him about his family and his single status. He told her about the bar that was pack owned that they made an effort to keep mostly human-free, so that they could talk and act naturally without worrying constantly about being overheard.

After dinner Hillary insisted that Theo let her do the cleaning up, then she called Zach.

"I miss you," he growled, without even saying hi.

She laughed. "I miss you too."

They talked for a long time, Hillary telling him all about Stephen, Zachary filling her in on pack business he had attended to that day. He told her about his work at the paper company. Finally, he told her that the National Alpha, Myra Talmidge from St. Louis, would be flying in on Thursday. She wanted to meet with them before flying to Arizona to meet with the alphas, William and Janet Sanderson.

Hillary couldn't believe how much she missed Zachary, though they'd been apart less than a day. Her voice must have gotten sad because Zach became comforting.

"It's normal, especially this soon after mating, to feel a separation anxiety. I'm really sorry I can't be down there tonight. I'm going to try to fix things to go down Tuesday night, instead of Wednesday, but I'm not really confident of that."

"I don't blame you. It's just so weird to go from happily being alone to needing you so badly."

"I know, baby, I feel it too. I'm just so happy that I have you in my life now. It's hard to believe that I didn't know you existed a week ago. I think I'm going to have to get Aaron some kind of extra-nice gift for finding you."

She smiled. "I owe him pretty big myself."

They dragged their goodbyes out to an embarrassingly teenager-like degree, before Hillary finally hung up, afraid she might get weepy if she didn't. She took a hot bath and said goodnight to Theo. After sleeping on her own for her entire life, she was amazed at how difficult she found it to go to sleep that night without Zachary there in her bed.

The next two days dragged on. Hillary survived by giving Zachary's table her complete attention, breaking only long enough to show the mayor the bed, which he heartily approved. She pretty much ignored Stephen and Alex as the two men tried to work around her without attacking each other. She knew that Alex had invited Stephen to dinner on Wednesday, ostensibly to meet Zachary. She could sense Alex getting more and more nervous, so she finally told him to take Stephen home early and expend some of his excess energy before coming to dinner.

Anthony and Theo were taking turns watching the house and the shop. Anthony was with her that afternoon. She skipped lunch, working hard on the table. It had become her labor of love and she hoped that Zachary liked it. She got more and more jittery as the afternoon wore on, however, and finally had to put her tools up about three o'clock.

As she was cleaning up she realized she could actually feel Zach coming closer through their bond. Once she realized that, and relaxed into the feeling, she became much calmer. She and Anthony headed out to the house.

Hillary had put a roast in the Crock-Pot before leaving the house that morning, and the wonderful aroma greeted her when they got home. She decided to take her time readying herself for her mate, something she'd never done before. She took a long bath then spent considerable time smoothing lotion over her body. She sent her feelings of joy and anticipation down the link to Zach and smiled to herself when she felt his response moving from eagerness toward desperation.

She put on the jeans that showed her ass off the best and a top that hugged her snugly and just barely reached the waistline of her jeans. Instead of her usual French braid she brushed her hair out smooth and added a bit of gel to keep it tame. She put on just a touch of makeup as she felt Zach coming closer.

It dawned on her that they weren't going to be able to keep from attacking each other. Biting her lip, she went into the living room to suggest that Anthony and Theo might want to take a long drive to get some beers for dinner or something. They had apparently anticipated her—Anthony was holding the keys to his car as they watched Zach pull up to her house.

"We're going to head out, run a few errands. We'll call before we come back, make sure there isn't anything else you want us to pick up," Theo said, opening the door.

ZACH NODDED BLANKLY at Theo and Anthony as they passed him, his focus completely on the woman standing in the hallway. He had a vague impression of an attractive yard and house, but paid little attention. What mattered now was Hillary and getting his hands on her. Immediately. Two steps through the doorway and Hillary launched herself at him. He would have laughed but their mouths were already tangled together and he only managed a gasp.

He slammed the door shut then braced himself against it, one arm supporting her delicious ass, the other tangled into her long hair. Finally he tore his mouth free.

"Bed. Where's the damn bed?" he panted.

Hillary dropped her legs and took Zach's hand, practically sprinting down the hall into her bedroom. She turned to him and started tearing off his clothes, while he did the same with hers. Their hands tangled up in each other until Zach took a step back.

"Faster this way." He began to remove his own clothes, his eyes glued to Hillary as she followed his lead and pulled her shirt over her head. She pushed her jeans and panties down so quickly she nearly tripped over herself but Zach was already finished and he steadied her then bent to complete the job. She unhooked her bra while he was at it, then they came together.

Hillary moaned as her hands roamed up his back and down to his buttocks. Her kiss was wild as he held her close, his hands gripping her hair, holding her to him as if she might slip away.

"I need you, Zach. I need you now." She pressed herself against his aching cock.

"Now. Always. Yours. *Mine.*" He pulled her onto the bed, landing with her on top.

She took the opportunity to run her hands over his chest and stomach, while his own came up to cup her breasts. His thumbs brushed her nipples and she returned the favor. They groaned in unison. She tweaked and pulled and he did the same, and Hillary cried out, a small orgasm taking her over. He watched for a second, loving the surprise and pleasure flashing across her face. Then he took advantage of her momentary distraction and reversed their positions.

Allowing some of his weight to press into her, he cradled his cock between her thighs, which immediately opened in invitation. He brushed her nipples with his chest, nibbled at her neck until she was clutching at him again, ready for more, needing more.

When she was bracing her legs on the bed and thrusting her hips at him, Zach surged inside her in one smooth thrust. The feeling of coming home was so intense, the love that surged through their shared bond so electric, they both came at once.

Damn, he'd missed her. Missed touching her and tasting her. Just being with her would have been enough, but being inside her...nothing had ever been like this, could ever come close to being like this. Zach rested his forearms alongside her head, his hands twisting in her hair. He leaned in and kissed her, gently this time. He teased her lips then traced her jaw, nipping and licking as he went. When he reached her earlobe and bit, she arched her hips and gasped, squeezing his dick, still hard inside her.

She moaned then fisted her hands in his hair, pulled his face back to hers, claimed his mouth as she rotated her hips as much as she could with his weight holding her down. He groaned into her mouth, moving his hands to her breasts while they kissed, but holding himself still inside her.

Hillary growled, pushing her hips up, but Zach growled back, biting her lip. She stilled as his hands caressed her breasts and his mouth went roaming again. This time he nipped the cleft of her chin then licked down her neck. She began to move again, bracing her feet against the bed to lever herself up, but he bent his knees, also rising so that she couldn't push farther onto him.

"Zach, *please*," she begged, then went still again as his mouth found the spot where her shoulder met her neck and he bit down. Peace like he'd never imagined spread through him, tinged with a slice of fear at the idea that he'd almost lost her before ever meeting her. Bad enough that they'd hurt her, but if they'd killed her...

But now wasn't the time for those thoughts. He released his gentle bite, licking the spot before returning to her face. Tears spilled down her cheeks, causing his heart to stutter. She projected only love and need, though, so he leaned down and tasted the salty sweetness.

Suddenly he reversed them again, so that she was on top, her tight walls sliding down his shaft. She leaned down to kiss him, bracing her hands beside his head so that she could increase her pace. His hips rose and fell with her rhythm and his hands moved down her back then came to rest at her waist.

He used his hands to help pull her down while he thrust deeply into her once, twice, before they froze and came together. Hillary collapsed on top of him, breathing heavily .

After a few minutes Zach carried her to the bathroom. He sat her down on the counter and leaned over to start the bathwater. He turned around and caught her staring at his backside. His cock twitched and he laughed.

"Baby, I don't think I can do you any justice right now." He came to her on the counter, his hands on her cheeks. "I missed you so much. I don't know if I can do that again." Hillary nodded and rested her forehead against his chest.

They got into the bath, Hillary lying against Zach, his arms around her. His fingers played idly with hers, then traced over her ring.

They'd discussed details for the wedding on the phone. Todd and Maria were helping her and they were keeping it small, but there was still some work to do. They talked about it now, trading ideas, dividing up the work. When the water started to cool, they climbed out.

"I like your house."

She laughed. "You've hardly seen any of it."

"True, but I liked what I've seen." He leered at her and she laughed again, smacking him with her towel.

"We need to let the poor guys know that they can come back."

They got dressed and called Theo and Anthony. Hillary blushed when he went to the front door and called for Brad to come inside. She'd obviously forgotten that he would be with Zach. It reinforced the need for having the guys around though, as she'd clearly not thought twice about sending her guards away when he'd gotten there. And they'd been much too busy to be aware of their surroundings for the last two hours.

When Theo and Anthony arrived, she reminded everyone that their guests, Todd, Maria and Stephen, thought this dinner was just about meeting Hillary's fiancé. After Todd and Maria left, they would talk to Stephen.

"It's scary," Zach said to Hillary when they were alone again in her room. "The idea that we have a part in someone else's feeling the same happiness that we are, but that it could go wrong. That we have some responsibility to see that it *doesn't* go wrong."

"I know, but like you said, they're feeling the same drive to bond that we have been, so there probably isn't much we need to do, other than help Stephen get over the shock." Her brow creased and she looked at him.

"You bit me, like you said a mate needs to do to make the change."

He shrugged. "It's a male wolf thing, I guess. I've never been driven to do it before." He came to her, pushed her shirt aside and licked the spot. She shivered and ran her hands up under his shirt.

Zach groaned and pulled away. "It wasn't enough, Larry, it's never enough with you. I need you again and again."

She smiled then kissed him quickly on the lips. "Oh, you'll have me, Zach, again and again. You're mine and I'm not letting you get away." She dragged him into the kitchen with her, where Anthony, Theo and Brad were talking.

"You said you would talk to Taylor about his conversion experience. What did he have to say?" she asked.

"He said that when Uncle Sam and Claire sat him down and told him they were werewolves, he thought they were kidding. Then he got nervous, thought maybe Claire was in some kind of freakish cult that he would have to rescue her from. The one thing he never thought was that he should leave her or get away. When she changed for him and he believed, the hardest part was worrying about the conversion. He wanted to put it off, have time to make a decision, but Uncle Sam pushed him, told him that he wouldn't be allowed to just date Claire, that it was an all-or-nothing thing. That pissed him off and he started to fight with Uncle Sam, but then he looked at Claire and she looked so sad, and he just gave in, right then—realized he was only fighting it out of fear, not because he was worried that he didn't love her."

Hillary frowned. "So the magic is definitely strong, because, really, that's pretty remarkable that he would just give in like that when he was afraid of becoming a wolf. I mean, what idiot would just agree to that, without wanting more time? Nobody would, without a strong influence."

Anthony agreed. "It's just as strong a drive for the human to go along with it, as it is for two wolves to mate, when they realize they're matched. I don't know why we would assume the magic would work more strongly on wolves than it does on humans. It's wolf magic, but it's chosen that person as a mate, chosen them to be a wolf."

"He's your friend, Larry. Do you think there's a particular way that we should go about this?" Zach asked.

"Well, he'll be thinking he's here to figure out if I'm crazy for wanting to marry you so quickly, and at the same time he'll be freaking out over the fact that he loves Alex already. Stee's a romantic, he'll love the idea that his strong feelings for Alex are justified and guaranteed to be returned. I mean, that's a total win for him."

She began to set the table, but the doorbell rang. Zach went with her and she introduced him to Todd and Maria, then Stephen when he arrived with Alex. They chatted for a few minutes then went right in to dinner.

DINNER WAS companionable as Hillary watched her friends get to know her pack. She could tell that they were pleased with the respect the guys showed her and the obvious affection Zach gave her. They talked about plans for the wedding and everyone ignored the way Stephen and Alex attempted to keep their hands to themselves.

They brought each other up to speed on what they'd been working on. Theo told Zach that he'd recommended a certain property to Hillary in Mountain View for her shop and she had Todd checking into it. Anthony knew of someone who might be interested in working with her and Stephen, but he couldn't tell Zach who it was, as it might reveal too much about her business. They all teased Zach about that. He knew now that she was working on a birthday present for him that Aaron had commissioned, but nothing specific.

Zachary insisted that he and his guys would clean up while Hillary allowed her friends to grill her in the living room. This earned a laugh from Maria and Todd, though Stephen was too occupied with Alex to appreciate the humor. When they were alone, Hillary was very conscious of the fact that the wolves could hear them clearly from the kitchen, but her friends were very sweet in congratulating her.

The kitchen crew came in after cleanup was completed and they shared a drink before Todd and Maria insisted they needed to get home. Stephen stood too, but Alex held him back as Zachary and Hillary escorted the married couple to the door and said goodbye.

When they came back in, Alex tugged Stephen back onto the couch and Theo, Anthony and Brad said their own goodbyes and left the room. Stephen looked a little surprised and nervous, giving Hillary a questioning look.

Alex cleared his throat. "Stee, there's something I need to tell you, something that will make the reason Hillary wants to marry Zach so quickly a bit more clear." He paused, glanced nervously at Hillary and Zach, who nodded at him reassuringly. "I told you I loved you yesterday and you said you loved me too." He waited for Stephen to acknowledge this.

Stephen, clearly uneasy with the turn of the conversation, nodded then blushed.

"My people," Alex continued, "have a way of knowing almost immediately if we've met the person we're meant to be with, the person who will love us as much as we love them. I knew the moment I met you that you were mine. Hillary did too, that's why she didn't worry about you running off with me so quickly. She recognized almost immediately that you and I have the same kind of bond that she had just found with Zach." He paused, letting Stephen absorb this.

Stephen looked confused. "Your people?"

Alex nodded and took a deep breath. "My people. Werewolves. There's a magic involved in being a werewolf and part of that magic is knowing when you've met your mate. Werewolf mates are for life, we love strongly and there's no going back once mated. You are my mate."

Stephen blinked. Swallowed. Blinked again. He turned to Hillary.

"Werewolf?" he asked, clearly expecting this to be some kind of joke.

She nodded. "I'm a werewolf, have been for four years. That's what I do when I take those long weekends to go camping by myself. I go out to the woods and run around as a wolf for a while, sort of recharge. If I go too long without changing, I become a cranky bitch and you tell me that I need to get laid. You had the right idea, just not the right solution."

Stephen's gaze bounced between Hillary and Zach, then back to Alex.

"You're saying you're all wolves."

Alex nodded. "Hillary and Zach met last week, and because they're both wolves, they knew right away that they were mates."

This time Zach nodded his agreement, bringing Hillary's knuckles to his lips for a kiss.

"And now you're all here because I'm Alex's mate and he loves me and that's why I have such strong feelings for him."

Alex gave a low growl. "Last night it wasn't strong feelings. Last night you said you loved me."

Stephen gave a small jerk at the growl, then grew angry at the reminder.

"Yes, well, that was before you told me that you weren't human! What the hell am I supposed to do with that bit of information? I don't believe in werewolves. Or magic!"

"But you believed that you loved him after only two days?" Hillary asked him gently. "You know I would never make something like this up, never try to hurt you. I'm so happy for you because I know that you've found true love that will last a lifetime, even if you don't know it yet. I'm happy that I don't have to keep a huge part of myself secret from you anymore, and that you get to experience the joy that I've felt since joining with my mate."

Stephen narrowed his eyes. "Okay, fine, yes, I love him, but I don't feel like I've joined my life with him."

Alex's eyes went challenging and Hillary rushed to speak before he could drag Stephen to the bedroom and show him a joining.

"That's because you aren't mated yet. You're feeling the attraction, the pull to become mated, but until you do, you won't feel joined. Alex is holding back, trying to let you catch up so that you can take that final step together. He's fighting his instincts because he needs you to understand what is happening and agree to it, and because it's law that he has permission to take that next step. He wants to mate with you, but that will turn you into a werewolf, like us."

Stephen stood up, and so did Alex. Stephen looked at Hillary, looked at Alex and sat back down, abruptly. "You're serious," he stated, sounding bewildered.

Alex cleared his throat. "Would you like..." he paused, took a deep breath. "Would you like to see my wolf?"

Hillary's heart ached to see her friend so confused, and to see her strong second scared. She knew it wasn't something that happened to Alex often. Hillary went to sit next to Stephen and Zach went to Alex, putting his hand on his shoulder to give him reassurance. Alex smiled gratefully, relaxing visibly under his alpha's support. Hillary smiled when Stephen narrowed his eyes at Zach's touching Alex.

Alex began removing his clothes and Stephen looked at Hillary in alarm. She smiled at him and gave Alex a leisurely inspection. She looked at Zach and smiled because now he was narrowing his gaze at her. She laughed and put her hand on Stephen's shoulder, feeling his muscles bunch.

When Alex was naked, Zach stepped away from him, holding his clothes. Alex took one deep breath and changed. He was nearly solid gray with just a touch of silver shot through. Stephen had stopped breathing and Hillary hugged him reassuringly until he took in a shuddering breath. She held her hand out to Alex who came to her gratefully, placing his muzzle in her hand, his eyes on Stephen.

Hillary scratched behind Alex's ears with her free hand and waited. At last Stephen inched his hand out to join hers on top of Alex's head. He plunged his fingers into the pelt. "Holy shit," he breathed, then jerked as Alex came closer to him, wiggling between his legs. Stephen's eyes were huge, his face pale, but he stroked the fur, his breathing settling. "Holy, holy shit."

Looking at Hillary in astonishment, the color beginning to return to his face, Stephen said, "You can do this too?"

Zach had come up to her other side, kneeling next to the couch, stroking Alex's side reassuringly. "She's the only white wolf I've ever met, very rare, absolutely gorgeous." Hillary blushed.

"He's pretty impressive himself." She gave Alex one last pat on the head.

Alex backed away and changed. Hillary could feel a thread of power pulsing between Zach and Alex and realized that Zach was sharing strength with Alex, helping him make the change, so that Alex wouldn't be too tired from making the change back again so rapidly.

Nodding his thanks at Zach, Alex took his clothes into the kitchen. He came back a minute later, dressed, eating an energy bar.

"Um," Stephen said. "So, you're werewolves."

They all laughed.

Alex knelt in front of Stephen again, pushing between his knees, taking his hands into his own. "Stephen, you're my mate and I want you to be with me. I promise that I will do everything in my power to make you happy in this life. I know it's asking a lot, but I have no choice, because I love you and you're mine. I want to give you time, but I have to tell you, the more we make love, the harder it is for me not to bite you. I don't think I can risk being with you until you're ready for that."

Hillary could hear Stephen's gulp. "Bite me?" His eyes had grown wide again.

"Not that kind of bite," she told him, glad that she was able to reassure him about this. "It's, you know, sexual. While you're having sex. It's a good thing, I promise." Now she blushed, and Zach ran his hand down her arm, which reacted with goose bumps.

"I would never hurt you," Alex added. "There's more that you should know, though. Becoming a wolf, being with me, would mean you would also be joining a pack. It's our community and there are laws and rules and leaders. I hold a position of power and you would be expected to share that with me. Hillary and Zachary are in charge, and they would have some power over you."

Frowning again, Stephen asked, "What do you mean, power over me?"

Alex thought about how to explain. "They are the alpha pair of our pack. They're in charge. While I hold a strong position and have my own power, the need to support them and the pack as a whole, is very strong. If one of them told me to do something that I didn't want to do, I would have to work very hard to resist the need to obey them. But since the need for them to do what is best for the pack is very strong, that would be very unusual. Zach has never told me to do something that I'm unwilling to do."

Hillary, who hadn't really had time to think through all the ramifications of pack power, was curious about this as well. "But if you wanted to, you could leave the pack. If the disagreement was that important to you."

Alex nodded. "Yes, but it would have to be very important. Probably, I would do what was asked, then leave. The order would have to be *extremely* wrong, like, I don't know, killing someone who I didn't think should be killed, before I would be able to just disobey and walk away. It's hard to say, exactly, because it's just not a situation I find myself in." He paused, rising to sit on the couch beside Stephen.

"Sometimes I need to do things I don't particularly want to do, but I know they need to be done just as much as Zach does. It's not a matter of disagreeing, just not liking something. Those cases are rare too, because Zach would feel my distaste and wouldn't ask me to do something like that unless there was no choice."

"Wait, don't you already know this stuff, Larry?"

"I've been a werewolf for four years, like I said, but I've never met a pack before Aaron introduced me to his wife and brother." She gestured to Zach. "Once Zach and I mated, he introduced me to the rest of the pack, so I'm learning all about it too."

Zachary stood up, pulling Hillary with him. "We'll give you guys some time to talk about things." He looked Stephen in the eyes. "We love Alex and are thrilled he's met his mate. We want to welcome you to our pack. I think you'll be happy as a part of our community and I look forward to getting to know you better."

Hillary and Zach went outside and chatted with Anthony, who they found watching the moon and stars. They joined him on the grass and talked until the front door opened up again. They went inside. Stephen and Alex were holding hands and though they both looked nervous, Alex smiled. Hillary suddenly broke out in a cold sweat, fear washing through her. Zachary and Alex reacted immediately, Zach pulling her behind his back, Alex moving to flank her, pulling Stephen with him.

"What? What's wrong?" Alex asked, his eyes searching. Zachary had already gotten over his initial reaction to her fear enough to sense what was going on. He turned around and pulled her into him.

"It's not the same, baby, I swear." He kissed her hair, rubbed her back. "They'll mate, no pain, I promise. Then tomorrow, we can all go out to the woods together. If he were regular pack, we would wait for the full moon, but since he's hierarchy, he'll feel better if he changes earlier, an outlet for the power that will be building. He might need our help, since the moon's not full, until he gets a handle on his power. One change now, then when the moon is full next week he'll be ready to run with the rest of the pack. No pain, no fear, maybe just a little nervousness."

She nodded against his chest, relaxing enough to feel Alex's anxiety. She realized that Stephen was reacting to her fear. "I'm sorry, Stee. Alex and Zach say your turning will be painless and I believe them. It's just that I wasn't turned by my mate, so it's different." She saw the connections forming as he remembered her hesitance with men and figured he'd drawn some fairly accurate conclusions. She would let Alex explain the rest to him later, but now they needed to focus on him.

She went to Stee and hugged him tight. "I'm so glad you're going to be as happy as I am. You deserve someone special and I had already decided Alex was special before I saw how you couldn't take your eyes off him." They laughed, Hillary glad to have cleared some of the fear from his eyes. "You guys go, you know, have a good time and all, and we'll see you tomorrow."

When they walked out the door, Hillary asked, "It's okay for them to leave? They shouldn't maybe do this here?"

"If they were regular pack I would stick closer but Alex is

powerful, so I know Stee will be too. They'll be fine. We'll be able to feel when the connection is made and we're close enough to get to them quickly if we sense any problems."

They took their time getting ready for bed, enjoying being together again while doing the simple things. They got under the covers and lay on their sides, facing each other, talking and touching. They felt the moment that Alex's bond with them flared brightly and changed, as it became forever entwined with Stephen's soul. They could feel the connection, distantly, to Stephen, and Hillary smiled at the thought of firming the connection the next day when she saw him.

They made slow, sweet love and fell asleep, wrapped up in each other's arms.

CHAPTER ELEVEN

Hillary was up bright and early the next morning, eager to see Stephen and see how he felt, to make sure that he was all right. She showed Zachary her office so he could work from there while she was at the shop. He would drive with Anthony to pick up the National Alpha and bring her to the house. Alex would bring Stephen so that after dinner they could go for his first run.

Knowing that Zach would be checking her outfit for clues as to what kind of shop she ran, Hillary purposefully dressed in her most raggedy jeans and t-shirt. She bounced up to him and gave him a loud kiss, smacked his ass and laughed her way out of the house. She could hear Brad trying not to snicker as he walked with her, having decided it was his turn to see her shop. Apparently the wolves were enjoying the fact that they knew what she did, but her mate didn't.

Hillary was giving Brad the quick tour when she felt Alex arrive with Stephen. She ran to him and hugged him hard, then stepped back, her hands on his face, to search for any signs of fear or distress. Seeing only happiness, she pulled his head down so she could kiss his forehead, then turned to hug Alex.

She turned back to Stephen who was looking a little shell-shocked, his hand covering his heart. He blinked up at her. "Wow, that's kind of weird." He rubbed at his chest a bit then dropped his eyes from hers. He breathed in deeply, trying to incorporate the new feelings rushing through him. Alex put an arm around his shoulders and Stephen leaned into the taller man.

"Stephen, I think this deserves our very best celebration!"

"You mean it?" he asked, a gleam in his eyes.

"Oh yeah, no doubt. You take Alex with you, make him help." She reached up to his face again, brushed his cheek gently. "I'm so glad you're with us. Now, hurry up, so we can celebrate."

Stephen took Alex's wrist and pulled him out of the shop while Hillary went to start work on Zach's table. Twenty minutes later she had to tear herself away to celebrate with the box of hot, glazed donuts that they returned with. When they'd indulged enough, she and Stephen got back to work.

Hillary worked through lunch, wanting to reach a certain point in the carving before breaking. At three o'clock she groaned and stretched, trying to work the kinks out. She left Stephen to finish what he was working on and she and Brad went back to the house. She showered and put on a dress, wanting to make a good impression on the visiting alpha. Theo had promised to make his beef Stroganoff again and she smelled its delicious aromas as she left the bedroom.

Stephen and Alex arrived and they talked about the upcoming transformation while they waited for Zach and Anthony to get there with their guest. She was a little bit nervous but trying to hide it. She hadn't asked Zach if Myra Talmidge was as powerful as they were and wasn't sure how she would react either way. She hoped that as with everything else since meeting Aaron, it would be natural and she wouldn't have to force any action on herself.

When they arrived, Hillary could feel the woman's power as she approached the house. She closed her eyes, concentrating on it. She thought that the woman was probably a little less powerful than she and Zach, but she had an added mantle of authority that Hillary sensed came from her position as National Alpha.

Hillary wondered if that just sort of appeared and disappeared when the position was transferred to the next alpha, or if it lingered. She would have to ask Zach later. For now, however, it definitely gave this woman a superior power to Hillary's and she realized that if she wanted to challenge this woman on anything, she would have to work at it. As it was, she found her head bowing slightly of its own accord as Zachary brought the alpha into the house.

"Alpha, this is Hillary Abbott, my mate. Hillary, this is Myra Talmidge, current National Alpha and alpha to the St. Louis Pack."

Hillary saw the woman's hand reach out to grasp her own, and felt the acceptance she had to offer. She looked into Myra's eyes and smiled.

"Hillary, I am so sorry we had to meet over such a troubling issue. I hope you'll consider my many years as alpha as a resource to you as you learn to navigate your way through our sometimes complicated world. You won't find so many wolves with a power equal to your own and I would be honored to be your friend and answer any questions you might have."

"Thank you—" Hillary froze, not sure how she should address the older woman.

Myra smiled. "Please, call me Myra."

"Thank you, Myra, it's good to know that I can ask someone other than these reprobates who I'm sure only tell me what they want me to know." She kept her face straight and Myra laughed. Turning, she introduced her wolves to Myra, who all dropped to their knees at the introduction. They went in to dinner and kept the conversation light for the meal. When it was over Zach, Hillary, Alex and Myra went into her office.

Myra began. "Hillary, I am sure that Zachary has told you that what you endured is so far outside our laws that we haven't even had to administer justice for such a case since I've been in hierarchy, about twenty-five years." She waited for Hillary to nod her acknowledgement.

"I've never heard of a pack alpha losing control of its territory to the extent that a rogue pack has formed. I'm sure things like that may have happened a hundred years ago, but not since we became organized and instituted National Council. There are a couple of things that I want to talk to you about before I tell you how we've decided to proceed."

She glanced around the table then focused again on Hillary. "I know that you're new to our ways, though you've been a wolf for four years. One of the reasons pack law is followed so carefully is that we, as a society, believe in swift and harsh judgment for all national crimes. There aren't a lot of national laws, but what laws do exist are for the purpose of protecting werewolves from humans, and humans from werewolves. In our experience it's very important that these laws be strictly enforced." She paused, leaned forward to put her hand on Hillary's.

"What I'm getting at is that we must deal much more harshly with lawbreakers than you're used to in human society. I'm sure that on the one hand you want severe retribution to these evil creatures who hurt you, but on the other hand I'm afraid that you won't approve of our means of administering that justice. There will be a trial, of sorts—we don't believe in summarily executing anybody—but it won't be what you're used to."

She leaned back, letting Hillary think about this.

"Zachary told me that the penalty for attacking a human is almost always death. You're right, to me that sounds extreme, like it should be more of a case-by-case basis, but it's not like you can just put the wolf in jail. I appreciate that you're sensitive to my feelings on this and I'll tell you that I'm glad I don't have to make the decision on their punishments. I feel comfortable in trusting Zach's opinion on what the council decides."

Myra nodded. "One of the reasons that we can make our decisions quickly and act decisively is that we have an enormous advantage that human courts don't have. That advantage will also mean that you won't be required to be present for anything that happens, if you don't want to be. That is, of course, the wolf and pack mentality. As long as the questioning wolf is powerful enough, they'll be able to demand answers from those being questioned and know that the truth is being told."

"I hadn't thought about that," Hillary admitted.

"So you can see, once we have them contained for questioning, it will be fairly simple to verify the truth of what they're up to. The trick, then, is in the containment. They'll know as soon as they see us that if they're caught, there's no lying, no playing dumb. No getting away with it. And they'll know there's little room for mercy when it comes to these laws. Containing them before they have a chance to run is the number one priority."

Alex nodded his agreement. "And right now we're basing everything on information that is four years old."

"Exactly," Myra said. "So we're going to do two things. I will go to Tucson and speak with the Sandersons, question them without telling them what's going on. I'll take the New York alpha, John Rodriguez, with me. He was an FBI agent. He works with a security company out there that has been allowed knowledge of werewolves. They've assisted us in the past, but mostly we've assisted them. John will choose a couple of the human operatives to go to Phoenix and do a reconnaissance, since it would be much more difficult for our wolves to do so without being scented.

"Once we figure out what the situation is, we'll make a plan to go in and capture the rogue pack, in total. We'll need members of some of the local packs to assist with that but I won't ask for Mountain Pack's participation. However, once they are contained, if you wish to, you may come see them while they're being questioned. The most important information we'll be focusing on first is determining if there are any other wolves out there that need our help, or any humans, for that matter."

Everyone nodded their agreement and Myra rose. "I know that you're joining your newest member for his first run. Would my company be intrusive?" she asked.

Hillary and Alex looked at each and shrugged their shoulders. "We'd welcome your presence, Myra. Thank you for coming here today."

ZACH COULD FEEL Stephen's nervousness as they walked back to the living room. He liked their new wolf and was looking forward to getting to know him better. He especially liked that Hillary would have one of her friends with her in Mountain View while she got to know the rest of the pack.

When they reached the living room, Stephen was pacing, with Anthony trying to soothe him, not very successfully. When he saw them, Stephen stopped and pasted on a smile.

Hillary laughed gently. "You're so cute when you're nervous," she teased, laughing again when he blushed. "Trust me, the hard part is over. Now all you have to do is enjoy the run." She took one of his hands and Alex took the other.

Zach squeezed his shoulder. "I know you're worried, you'd be crazy not to be. But it will be all right, I promise. In fact, it will be pretty spectacular." He put a touch of reassuring power behind the words, helping the poor man to relax.

Alex kissed Stephen gently and led him out to the cars. Zach took Hillary's hand and followed them.

They drove to Hillary's favorite campsite and headed off into different directions to change. Hillary and Zachary stayed close to Stephen and Alex, though out of sight. They could hear Alex murmuring encouragement and felt Stephen start to change, felt Alex give Stephen a pulse of power to help him along, although he probably didn't need it. When they knew he was wolf, they changed quickly and went to greet him.

Zach loved to watch Hillary run with their pack. She had tried for so long to be solitary, despite the friends who had worked their way into her heart. Seeing her now, playing with the guys, racing with Myra, was beautiful to him. They ran for a few hours then gathered back together. Hillary, Zach and Myra went to their clothing and changed back. They all piled into the SUVs and returned to Hillary's house.

The wolves camped out on the living room floor, and while

Hillary remade the guest bed for Myra, Zach pulled some items he'd purchased from his duffel bag and put them in the shower behind the shampoo and conditioner bottles. He started the water running, but waited for Hillary to join him. Zach soaped up his hands, getting a good lather. He applied it to her breasts lavishly, loving the slippery feel of her under his hands. When she was panting, he got a fresh layer of soap and moved down to her butt, giving each globe the same attention he had to her breasts.

"Baby," he whispered, pulling her cheeks apart and squeezing.

"Hmmm."

"At the cabin. Did you like it when I put my finger in here?" He swiped one sudsy finger over her asshole.

"I would have told you if I didn't."

"That's good." He smiled into her hair. She'd leaned forward, resting her head against his shoulder as he massaged her ass.

"I went shopping," he told her.

"Yeah?"

"Yeah." He took his hands away and rinsed them in the water, then pulled the lube he'd bought down from the ledge. She didn't move, even when he flipped the cap open with a plasticky pop. He poured a fair amount on his fingers and returned to her hole.

Her head came up when his slick finger pressed into her, just slightly. "You bought lube?"

"Yup," he answered, teasing the entrance until she pressed into him. He slid the finger in all the way.

"Oh." It was more of a gasp than a word.

"You like?"

She laid her head back in his shoulder. "Mmm-hmm."

He smiled in anticipation. He added more lube and then a second finger.

"Ah." She lifted her head again, going up on her toes before settling back down again.

"Still okay?"

She took a deep breath and he was able to slide into her more freely.

"Yes."

He moved his lips to her ear so that he could whisper enticingly, "Turn around."

She blinked up at him then slowly turned around and braced her hands against the wall, his fingers never losing contact. He added more lube and scissored the two fingers until she was moaning. With his other hand, he tested to make sure her pussy was still good and wet. Oh yeah. He had no idea how much hot water they had left. He needed to move this out of the shower.

Still working the two fingers, he reached behind the shampoo for his other purchase. The medium-sized butt plug had looked small in the store compared to some of the others, but now it seemed pretty big. He compared it to the width of his two fingers, and then to the width of his cock. Should be okay, and he would go slowly.

"Zach," she cried when he pulled his fingers free.

"Just a second, baby. I bought something else."

She turned her head but he'd already lubed the plug and had it resting against her rear. He pushed in slowly and she pushed out. The tapered end slipped in easily, followed by the first large bump. The next bump seemed stuck for a minute and he waited.

"Oh," she said, then bore down.

"One more, baby."

Her groan was all pleasure, he had no doubt.

"Fuck, that's hot," he said as the plug slid in to its base. He brought his hand around to her front and wasn't the least surprised to find her as wet as ever.

"Okay?" he asked, pulling down the bottle of shampoo.

She was still leaning against the wall but turned her to look at him. "Umm. That's it?" she asked.

He massaged the shampoo into her hair. "Well, we need to wash."

Conditioner came next and then she did the same for him. He noticed that she directed the hot water onto her neck for a while, bringing her hand up to work the muscles. He brushed her hand aside and replaced it with his own. Her muscles were tight.

"Why so tense, baby?" he whispered. "Are you worried about Arizona?"

"No, I was just working in an awkward position most of the day. I didn't move around as much as I should have." She groaned as his hands stopped their kneading while he contemplated her answer. He stepped back and swatted her butt, ignoring her shriek.

"Come on, dry off and I'll give you a massage."

"But what about..." She waved her hand vaguely behind herself and he had to grin.

"What about it? Is it bothering you?"

"No, but—"

"Will it be in the way of a massage?" he asked.

She gave him a dirty look, grabbed a bottle of lotion from the medicine cabinet and stomped past him.

Zach laid a clean towel on the bed and motioned her onto it. He started at her feet, massaging the arches, kneading the ball, working the toes. She tried to keep her moaning to a minimum, knowing the wolves could hear her easily, but gave up when he left her feet and moved to her shoulders. He worked the knots for a while until she was completely relaxed, then he changed his focus.

The kneading became more of a caress and he let his fingers curve to her breasts. Hillary's breathing picked up and she kept wiggling. He massaged her butt, working the flesh around the plug, then her upper thighs, circling around but avoiding her pussy .

"Please, Zach, please. I need you."

"You have me, baby, I'm all yours."

"Inside me, Zach, I need you inside me." She tried to turn over but he pressed down on her back. He pushed on her thighs and she eagerly spread them wide for him. One hand stayed on her back, his other hand testing her wetness. She was dripping.

"Zach, I'm ready, I swear, I need you inside me!" Her voice was rising and he hushed her gently. He gripped her hips and pulled her up onto her knees. He rubbed his hands over the firm globes of her butt, watched as one hole clenched in empty need while the other worked the rubber toy.

He swirled his cock through her cream, then pushed carefully inside. Fuck, she was tight. His dick rubbed along the bumps of the plug. They both moaned. Lying over her, he rested all his weight on one hand and used the other to massage her clit. She came around him, shuddering, but he gritted his teeth and held back. When she relaxed her grip on him, he pulled out. She started to lie down but he stopped her.

"Oh no. We're not done yet."

"We're not?" She sounded tired but interested.

"Nope."

He took the base of the plug between his fingers and gave it a jiggle. She groaned then panted as he began to pull it out, one bump at a time. She whimpered.

"What's the matter, baby?" he asked with a smile, rubbing his hands along her hips and ass.

"Zach."

"Right here," he assured her.

She wiggled her butt at him.

"I thought maybe you wanted to stop," he teased. "Zach," she growled.

He had the lube again and was applying a healthy amount to his cock, but she couldn't tell that. Her head hung between her arms and her eyes were closed. The sight was heart-stoppingly beautiful. He leaned down and licked her, from tailbone to as far as he could reach, needing to taste her. Salty and sweet, exactly right.

Kneeling upright again, he brought his cock to her back hole. As soon as he touched her, she surged back, trying to get him in. He held her steady with one hand on her hip while his other hand gripped his shaft. Inching his way inside, he closed his eyes against the incredible feeling of tight heat.

"Oh fuck, baby."

"More, Zach. I need more."

There was only one way to answer that. He gave her more. When he was seated balls-deep, he paused. She clenched tight around him and that was it, he couldn't hold back anymore. He thrust in slowly, but hard and deep, again and again, as she pushed back for more, until he came with a long groan, feeling like it lasted for an hour. He slid two fingers into her pussy and she fluttered against them.

She was mostly asleep when he carried her into the bathroom. He cleaned his lady, the toy and himself, and carried her back to bed. If they moved at all the rest of the night, he wasn't aware of it.

THE NEXT MORNING when Hillary got up early to make breakfast for Myra, Zach and Brad before they headed back to the airport, she was a little sore. And a little bit embarrassed about what the others must have heard. They made no mention of it and nobody gave her any funny looks, so she put it out of her mind. They spent a nice breakfast getting to know each other, Myra telling them stories about Uncle Sam's times on the council. When they left she roused the rest of the wolves and they made their plans for who should go where that day.

Hillary and Stephen worked hard on Friday so that they could go back to Mountain View with Zach and the others for a long weekend. She figured they could go and see the property that Theo had recommended, as well as scouting out any competition in the neighboring towns, and start a plan for moving the shop. They ran late but got a lot done.

When she got home she, Stephen and Theo immediately felt the tension in the house. Zach took her hand and led her to the kitchen table and they all sat down.

"Myra called. The Mesa hierarchy folded pretty much the minute she walked through the door. Turns out this Ken Cage is William Sanderson's nephew. Apparently when he was young, early twenties, he wanted to challenge the alphas and he was strong enough, and they were weak enough, that he might have managed it. So they got him to go to Phoenix instead. Myra's take is that they knew he was...off. It wasn't just a matter of his being young, they knew he was bad news to be in charge of their pack."

Hillary kept her eyes on the table. Zach had her hands in his. Alex got up to stand behind her and massage her shoulders and Stephen sat on her other side, his leg brushing hers.

"Keep going," she said, wanting to hear it all, get it behind her.

"They started hearing things a few years ago and have pretty much been waiting for the axe to drop. Apparently most of the pack is aware that there's a problem, though probably no one is sure of exactly what he's doing out there." Zach's voice was becoming a growl. "They chose to remain ignorant so that they wouldn't have to deal with the problem." He took a deep breath.

"Rodriguez's people started digging in Phoenix while Myra was here, to see what they could find. Apparently the locals consider the group a cult, which is really not far off. The whole group lives on the ranch and they don't go into town much. I'm not sure how they support themselves. Local law enforcement has been keeping an eye out, trying to catch them at something, but they haven't been successful. There've been a few missing persons that they want to pin on Cage but that might just be wishful thinking on their part."

"I think we should go out there," Hillary said, her eyes meeting Zach's.

"Myra and Rodriguez are landing in Phoenix about now. There's no sense doing anything until we hear from them."

"We can pack and be on the road. We need to head that way to go back to Mountain View, anyway. If we haven't heard from her by the time we get close to home, we can call her. Then we'll know if it makes sense to just stop at home or keep on going to the airport."

Zach nodded and they all got up to pack. While she put things into a bag, Zach watched her.

"I don't think you should go. What good will it do but bombard you with painful memories?" he finally said.

"I want to know it's over, need to know they've been stopped."

He came up behind her, wrapped his arms around her waist and leaned down to rest his chin on her shoulder. "Baby, people are going to die. Plus, with the cops watching, it's going to be dangerous, figuring out a way to handle everything without arousing more suspicion."

"I want to help. You've said it before, you and I are more powerful than most wolves. We can help."

"The National Council will send in whoever it needs to. There's just no reason to put yourself through this."

She turned around in his arms, kissed his lips. "Zach, baby, don't you know? Nothing will hurt me there as long as you're with me."

Zach groaned, rested his forehead against hers. "Fuck, Larry, you can't say things like that. It's not fair."

She smiled. "It's not about fair. I'm not asking you to understand why I need to be there. I'm not even sure I understand. It's enough that I feel very strongly that I should go, and that I know you'll go with me." She gave him a quick kiss on the cheek and went back to her bags.

The two cars were on the road within half an hour. They'd been driving for an hour when Zach's cell phone rang. It was immediately obvious that the news wasn't good, so Theo pulled the car over, Brad following suit behind them while Zach growled in the front seat.

"We're on our way to the airport now," was all he said before hanging up.

"They think a Mesa Pack member warned Cage. There's been some activity at the ranch. Rodriguez thinks that because the pack was pretty much waiting for the shit to hit the fan, when Myra showed up they didn't even wait to see why she was there, some fucker called and warned Cage right away."

"Shit!" Alex nearly shouted. "We should have considered that. How often does the National Alpha show up at some rinky-dink pack like that?"

Zachary gave Hillary a questioning look, clearly hoping she would change her mind. She put a hand on his shoulder. "They may need us. There may not be time for the help they need to get across the country."

He just closed his eyes and nodded, then got back on the phone to call Molly and fill her in. When they neared Mountain View, Hillary pointed out that not everyone had to go and asked Zach if they shouldn't ask for volunteers. She didn't feel comfortable asking the men to risk themselves. He just laughed and told her if she wanted to insult them she would have to do it herself. Theo, who was driving, was clearly in agreement, so Hillary let it go.

CHAPTER TWELVE

The flight was short and tense, everyone wishing they could just get there so they would know what was going on. When they landed there was a message from Myra that they should meet up with the Los Angeles wolves who would be waiting for them at the rental car counter, having recently arrived themselves.

"L.A. has a good pack," Zach told Hillary and Stephen as they walked. "Their alpha, Janet Washington, just mated last year. I haven't met him."

"My brother is in L.A.," Brad said. "He told me they have a high percentage of ex-military."

This was proven to be true as they saw a group of ten wolves waiting for them with barely concealed impatience, obviously itching to join the fight.

As they approached, he scanned the other group, narrowing on the most powerful pair, a man and woman who detached themselves and walked toward them. They were obviously conducting a scan themselves and narrowed their focus immediately on Hillary and Zachary.

The pair nodded their heads respectfully.

"Alpha."

Zach put out his hand to the woman, who was in front of him, while Hillary took the man's offered hand.

"I'm Zach, this is Hillary. We're alphas of Mountain Pack, in Idaho."

"I'm Rhonda and this is Trent, we're first in L.A. Pack. We have the paperwork all taken care of, if you're ready to go."

"Thank you, the faster, the better," Zach said.

As they walked, Trent introduced the rest of the group. When there was a lull in the conversation, Hillary asked a question which should have occurred to Zach.

"Did Jeff Cage...uh, what do you call it?" She looked at Zach. "When he was in L.A. for college, did he inform your pack?"

"He did," Rhonda answered. "He came to run with us a few times for the full moon and then disappeared. We found out he'd dropped out of school, so we checked with his alpha and were told he'd returned home. We didn't think anything about it."

Zach squeezed Hillary's hand and she smiled at him reassuringly. They got into the cars and started driving to the motel that John Rodriguez had set up as the staging point. They were nearly there when Hillary's cell phone rang. She checked the display.

"It's Myra," she told them as she answered, putting the phone on speaker. "Hello?"

"Hillary, this is John Rodriguez. How far out are you guys?"

Theo, who was driving, answered, "Close. Five to ten minutes."

"We have a situation. When you get to State Street, don't make the turn onto Third to come to the motel. Let your other car know. Myra is calling the L.A. cars. We have a sniper firing at the motel."

"Shit, is anyone hurt?"

Zach pulled out his phone and dialed Alex. He spoke quietly, updating his second quickly while listening to Rodriguez's answer.

"One of my wolves is down, but he's alive. I feel pretty confident this particular asshole is the asshole we want. The question is, is he alone."

"And I'm the only person who would recognize him. The L.A. group said they'd met Jeff, the nephew, but I didn't think to ask if anyone actually here remembered what he looks like. Can you check on that? Maybe you can send that group to the ranch house to work on the situation there, while our group handles your situation."

He could hear John relay the question to Myra. While they waited for an answer, Hillary turned to look at Zach. He didn't try to hide what he was feeling. He was worried about bringing her closer to gunfire, and though he managed not to say it, she would know that he was thinking it. She reached over and held his hand, which he found absurdly comforting. He wished he could just handle all this for her and tell her when it was over. She'd said she needed to do it herself, which he understood. Mostly. But he didn't have to like it.

"At least two of the L.A. wolves say they'd recognize Jeff. I'm sending them over to the ranch to see what they can observe, but telling them to hold the perimeter for now. I'm going to call your security guy and tell him I want your people to ease up on our position, see if they can confirm a location for the sniper and a number. Is that all right with you?"

"Yes, of course. Have the police responded yet?"

"Not so far. We're monitoring the radios and there've been no reports. There's only been the one shot. I don't think people realized what it was. We're on the outskirts of town here, not a lot of homes. That won't last if there are further shots, though. We need to get this guy down or we're going to have a hell of a mess on our hands."

"John, we're pulling over right now. I'll just put Alex on this phone for you." She hopped out of the car and handed the phone to Alex, then joined Zach in trying to see what they could make out. They realized quickly that John had stopped them far enough back from the scene that they wouldn't be able to tell what was going on from there. They went back to Alex to discuss the next move.

Handing the phone back to Hillary, Alex told them the plan. "Anthony and I are going to move around to where John thinks the sniper is. If we can get a visual and are sure that there are no backup positions, we'll bring Hillary in for an ID. If it's not Cage, we'll send more people out to the ranch. If it is Cage, John thinks bringing him down quickly will eliminate any resistance at the ranch."

Everyone nodded. Zach gave both men stern looks and told them to be careful. Alex gave Stephen a quick kiss and they were off.

Hillary took Stephen's hand. "This isn't exactly the honeymoon you had planned, is it?"

He swallowed hard. "The real pisser is I don't really even know much about this side of him. I don't know what his training and skills are."

"He's very good at this, Stephen," Zach said. "He was an Army Ranger for a lot of years and has been running the security company for five years. He has excellent instincts and he and Anthony have worked together. They make a good team."

Stephen nodded, still looking worried.

Hillary had the phone still connected with John, though she'd taken off the speaker. Zach gave her a questioning look and she handed it to him without complaint. "Any word from the ranch?" he asked John.

"They just got there. They're spreading out to cover the exits. I don't want any wolves leaving. No word on specific sightings yet."

His own phone buzzed and he and Hillary read the tiny screen together. He read it out for John. "Alex sent a message. It reads '2 young, probable trap'." He listened to John for a minute then nodded. "Okay." He handed the phone back to Hillary. "John thinks someone is watching this guy's position, waiting for us to take him out, then opening fire himself. Alex knows his stuff. He'll find the second shooter."

They waited for what seemed like forever before Alex suddenly appeared down the street, loping toward them.

"I found a spot where you should be able to see him without him smelling you," he told Hillary without preamble. "I think it's probably him."

"And if it is?" Hillary asked.

"Simple," Zach said, his smile fierce. "We tell him to put the gun down and come out with his hands up."

Hillary blinked. Seriously? "That seems a little bit too easy. You're saying because we're stronger than him he'll have to obey? Wouldn't he have thought of that?"

"He's crazy. He probably thinks nobody has enough power to do that, but we know he's a loon. Our combined power will mow him down, I have no doubt about that."

Zach seemed so confident of his answer that Hillary didn't bother getting nervous, just shrugged her shoulders. "Works for me." She brought the phone still connected to John up to her ear. "That work for you?"

"Yes. Alex is strong enough to take the first shooter at the same time? Either with power or just plain strength?"

"Yes," Hillary answered, not even needing to ask. Alex was clearly raring and ready to go. She handed the phone over to Theo and followed Alex, Zachary at her side.

As they made their way to the position Alex had chosen, Hillary tried to keep her breathing even but wasn't entirely successful. Zach squeezed her hand and she was just thankful she had him by her side. If she'd needed to confront the Cages before meeting Zach, she wasn't sure she'd have been able to handle it. Now, though she was nervous, she was nowhere near the basket case she probably would have been.

Alex led them to a building then backed them against the wall. He demonstrated that if they eased around the corner and looked up, they should be able to see the waiting shooter.

Zach looked at Hillary, clearly conflicted, but she just smiled at him. She got on her knees and peeked around the corner, which meant that Zach was able to look as well from above her. He rested one hand on her back and she felt the warmth all the way to her heart.

Looking up, Hillary's breath caught. She had seen that face in her nightmares. She was never sure who she hated more, Ken or Jeff. Now that she knew what it meant to be an alpha, to be in charge of the wellbeing of a pack, she knew that she hated Ken more. Somehow he had managed to corrupt the entire family.

Pulling back from the corner, Hillary looked at Zach and Alex and nodded. Alex sent a quick text to the others and they backed away far enough that they could whisper and not have the other wolf hear them.

Alex pointed out where they could stand and address Cage and still have cover if things went badly. "I'm going to leave Theo and Anthony here to help. Once you make your move, I'll take down the shooter."

Hillary narrowed her eyes at him. "You need to take one of the guys."

He was about to argue, but the very alpha looks he received from both Hillary and Zachary meant that he couldn't. He nodded his acquiescence and moved back to make the arrangements.

Zachary pulled Hillary into a hug, taking in a lungful of her scent. "Larry, will you let me do this?"

"Yes, but I'll be by your side."

He pulled back, rolling his eyes. "I suppose that's the best I'm going to get." He kissed her hard then steeled himself as Theo joined them. "She's your responsibility for this, Theo. You keep her safe no matter what she says to you." Zach's voice was all alpha.

"Yes, Zach."

Hillary gave them both dirty looks and started for the corner. They flanked her immediately. Once they had eased themselves into position, Zachary looked Hillary in the eyes and took a deep breath. She mirrored him then nodded. They faced the shooter, who was turned sideways to them.

Hillary held Zach's hand and willed her power into him. She felt him swell and flex his power as he prepared to speak.

"Ken Cage. Put down the gun and stand with your hands in the air. NOW." Hillary could practically see the power the words carried and she could definitely see the effect they had on the man they were watching.

As if in slow motion and clearly against his own will, the man lowered his gun. His arms trembled but the gun finally dropped from his hands to the ground.

"Hands in the air." There was a definite growl to Zach's voice now and Cage's hands rose, moving faster to comply this time. She could see the motel room door open across the way and saw Myra and a man she assumed was John Rodriguez step out. They began to walk slowly toward Cage from his front, while Hillary, Zach and Theo moved in from his side.

As they got closer they could see the sweat pouring from the man as he fought the compulsion to obey.

"On...your...knees," Zachary said, almost softly. They edged around so they could see his face more clearly. The menace in Zach's voice, combined with the power, gave Hillary goose bumps. Theo moved in behind the man to kick the gun out of his reach.

As the evil from Hillary's nightmare dropped to his knees, she saw his face clearly. The insanity was somehow clear now, as it hadn't been when she'd met him. She wondered if that was a gift of her wolf senses or if he had just gotten that much crazier in the last four years.

She saw the moment he realized who she was, saw the hatred flash through his face, as well as the moment of triumph. She kicked him in the face to wipe it off. Nobody moved as he hit the ground then dragged himself back up to his knees, his mouth and nose bleeding.

"How many humans have you attacked and attempted to convert?" Myra asked, and Hillary was amazed at the power that washed from the woman.

"Eight," Cage answered through gritted teeth, his whole body trembling now as he fought the power.

"How many lived?" John asked.

Cage glanced at Hillary. "T-two," was forced out.

"Who were they and what happened to them?" Hillary asked, letting her fury fuel her power.

"You, Jeff's slippery bitch," he sneered, then gasped in pain as every alpha there struck him with their power at the same time.

"You...we thought you were dead, but then you were gone. We followed for two days but never found you, so I told them you were lying dead in the woods somewhere, probably already eaten by other wolves." He swayed then his eyes flashed. He started to turn, obviously deciding the only way to get out of answering their questions was to become a wolf.

Again Hillary could feel the combination as they all forced his wolf to recede. Cage gasped, pain etching his face as the transformation was halted and reversed.

"Tell us the rest," John commanded.

Cage was panting now. "Before *her* there was a man. My sister wanted him. I didn't think he would make it, he didn't look very strong. Once he turned, I realized he was too strong, so I shot him, but he got away."

"Tell us more."

"He was from town, a teacher or something, I don't remember his name."

John stepped forward, pulling something out of his pocket. "Turn. Now." Immediately the man became a wolf, his tail between his legs, his belly on the ground, his head between his paws. John shook out the item in his hand, a choke collar and leash. The wolf whimpered.

John growled at him as he bent down and secured the collar and leash, then dragged the wolf behind him to an SUV, putting him into the back.

Zach pulled his phone out and directed Brad and Stephen to bring the cars to them. Alex came up with a rifle in one hand and the arm of a very subdued Jeff Cage in the other. Jeff was hunched over, his eyes firmly fixed to the ground. Alex pulled him to a stop in front of the group. Zachary reached over and yanked Jeff's head up by the hair.

"Look at me, scum." Jeff's wide eyes reluctantly but instantly met Zach's. Every inch of Zach's face showed his disgust, and tears began to fall from Jeff's eyes. Hillary felt only revulsion and turned to talk to Myra. Alex took Jeff into the motel room and left him to be guarded by one of John's wolves.

"So, we take Cage to the ranch and the other wolves just walk out?" Hillary asked the alpha.

"Exactly."

"Then what do we do with them?"

Myra looked at her calmly. "It will be my job to determine which wolves can be rehabilitated and moved into packs with strong alphas willing to take them on."

Hillary thought about that for a minute. "That's not a job I would want."

"But if it were yours, I've no doubt you would see to it as justly as possible."

Bowing her head at the compliment, Hillary wrapped her arms around herself. "This seems...sort of anticlimactic."

Myra nodded. "It's one of the reasons this kind of thing never—well, rarely, I guess we have to say—happens. When all it takes is someone with the power to tell you to stop, it's supposed to be harder to get away with evil. What this insane group of wolves has allowed to go on here is truly abhorrent, but I'm almost more upset with the supposedly sane members of Mesa Pack who allowed it to continue." She turned and looked at the wolf in the SUV. "One phone call. That's all it would have taken to stop this. Just one damn phone call." She shook her head. "Believe me, I'll be spending quite a bit of time in Tucson breaking that pack up."

"If there's anything we can do, you know that we'll be happy to help."

Myra laughed. "Hillary, you're going to be a true joy to watch as you learn the ways of our people. I have a feeling you and your mate will grow quite a bit more powerful before you're done."

They got into the cars that pulled up and made their way to the ranch.

As they neared, Hillary let the memories of that long-ago drive wash through her. Zachary held her tight beside him and she knew that he could feel the pain she conjured up, but knew also that he could feel how she had healed, with his help.

When the cars came to a stop she made no move to get out,

Zachary staying with her. She leaned her head against her mate and sighed.

"Myra was right, this was all such a waste." She watched through the windshield as John pulled the very meek wolf from the SUV. The big man walked the wolf forward, allowing no slack in the leash held tightly in his hands. The cowed wolf kept his tail tucked between his legs and his head low.

She couldn't hear what was going on outside but she could feel the tension as the Mountain View and Los Angeles wolves spread out to contain the wolves on the property. She heard Myra's muffled voice, full of power, call out, commanding the wolves to her presence. They came, meekly, not even attempting to fight the power of Myra's command. Hillary realized that they had felt the moment when their chosen alpha had given in and they had no will of their own to fight.

She saw Jeff's parents and couldn't even summon anger, only disgust. One by one, as the wolves reached the driveway where Myra and John stood, with Cage on his belly before them, the Phoenix wolves dropped to their knees and bowed their heads.

"Will they do it here? Now?" Hillary asked.

"Yes. They'll want all the wolves who gave him their loyalty to see that he's dead."

"I don't need to watch. Let's walk." She felt his hesitancy, realized that part of him *did* want to watch, wanted to see her enemy suffer, but he got out of the car and came around to her side. Taking her hand he let her lead him away from the house, to an outbuilding, like a separate garage.

When she felt him stiffen beside her, Hillary at first thought it was because he felt her fear at facing the room where she'd been raped. But then she, too, caught the scent. Life.

"Alex." Zach's voice was quiet and Hillary realized that since they had stepped out of the car Alex had been close behind. It gave her pause to realize how involved in her memories she had been, as well as how much she trusted Zach and his wolves to watch her back, allowing her to lower her own guard, even in this place that haunted her.

Alex gave a low growl as he too smelled the human. Hillary concentrated and detected fear and despair, sweat and dirt, but no sex smells. She took a deep breath and resumed her route to the cell-like room she'd been kept in for four days.

Alex sped up his pace so that he would arrive before them. Hillary let him open the door, let Zachary edge his body in front of hers. When she realized what she was sensing, however, she pushed past them, growling low when they moved to stop her. They backed off and Hillary entered the room.

It was hard to see as the gray light of dawn filtered into the room. Hillary reached to the wall switch she remembered, turning on the single light. In the far corner was a human girl. Hillary guessed her to be around eight. There was a tray with an empty cup and bowl just inside the room, next to the door. A mattress was on the floor, with a blanket. The girl had her knees drawn up in front of her, her faced tucked into her knees. Her very dirty hair was probably brown, though Hillary couldn't be sure, but her eyes, just barely visible behind the hair and knees, were bright green. Hillary entered the room slowly, projecting as much calm reassurance as she could manage. Those green eyes remained fixed on her, but the girl made no sound or movement.

"Alex, send word to Myra and John," Zach murmured.

Hillary came within a couple of feet of the girl and sat down, bending so that they were at eye level.

"Hello. My name is Hillary. These guys are Zach and Alex."

The silence was very loud, the girl's eyes unblinking on Hillary until Zach stepped into the room, then they blinked and ducked back down behind her knees. Zach came and sat next to Hillary. He looked around the room and shuddered then put his arm around Hillary.

Zach kept his voice low and even. "Do you know the people who live here?"

The girl gave no sign that she understood.

Hillary tried, "We want to take you away from here. The people aren't good, as I'm sure you know, and we came to make them leave. Can you tell us your name and where your home is, so we can take you there?"

Hillary's breath caught as she could just make out two tears sliding down the girl's cheek. She felt Zach's tension, knew it came from the idea of returning this girl without knowing what she'd seen and heard from the wolves, but he made no comment.

"We want to help you. Will you let us?"

The tears began to flow freely from the girl and Zach's arm tightened around Hillary as they both felt the spark of hope in the girl flare to life. Hillary had to swallow the lump in her throat as she slowly reached her hand out to lay it on the child's head.

When Alex came back only moments later, Hillary was holding the sobbing child, while Zach had his arms wrapped around them both. They sat that way until the girl fell asleep in her arms then gently lifted her.

Stepping out into the early morning light, Hillary saw that Ken Cage was dead. His wolf's body was lying bloody on the driveway. The rest of the Phoenix pack was sitting in a loose grouping, with a couple of the L.A. wolves standing watch. Hillary started walking to the house and knew the moment her wolves and the L.A. wolves scented the human child and realized what she was holding. The tension level skyrocketed and she heard low growls from many directions. All of the Phoenix wolves lowered themselves further to the ground.

The girl whimpered and Hillary soothed her while Zach made a silencing gesture to the wolves. Hillary felt them actively tamping down their rage so as not to frighten the girl she carried into the house. Myra stepped away from where she was talking to John, Trent and Rhonda. She motioned them inside. "I asked your Stephen to run a bath."

Hillary nodded her thanks and went inside. She had only to think of Stephen to be able to follow her link to him and know where he was. Zach went with her to the master bedroom, and he and Stephen waited there while she bathed the girl. She woke up and seemed very happy for the bath, but still didn't speak. Hillary wrapped her in a clean fluffy towel and left her on the floor while she went into the bedroom. Stephen handed her a t-shirt and sweatpants.

"These were the smallest I could find." Hillary held them to her nose, ensuring that they smelled only of laundry soap, not of any of the Cages. She took the clothes into the bathroom and helped the girl dress.

She took a brush and the girl's hand and led her into the bedroom, sitting with her on the bed, and began brushing her hair. She could see in the mirror over the dresser that the girl kept her eyes down, seemingly at ease with them. She stiffened just slightly before Alex came into the room then relaxed again.

"I've made up the spare bedroom with clean sheets," Alex reported. Hillary could tell from his expression that he had some news. She finished brushing the girl's hair dry, and marveled that the dirty mess she had seen earlier was now a rich auburn. Leading her down the hall, Hillary tucked her into bed.

"Would you like one of us to stay in the room with you while you sleep?" Hillary asked.

Small eyebrows knitted for a moment, then smoothed. The tiniest of nods was like a triumphant shout to Hillary and she smiled hugely.

"We'll take turns, if that's okay with you. Maybe Stephen could start?" There was no reaction from the girl so Hillary left Stephen in the room with the door open. They stood out in the hallway, everyone listening for the sounds of steady breathing, which they soon heard.

Whispering, Alex told them what had been discovered in the questioning of the wolves. "Apparently Cage went on a trip eight months ago, and came back with the girl, who he called Alexis." His voice was growing louder in agitation, and they heard a whimper from the bedroom, so they moved back to the master bedroom,

Hillary and Zach both putting their hands on him to help him calm down.

"At first, she lived in this house with the Cages for about two months. But she kept crying and screaming for her mommy and daddy, kept trying to run away. It got so they were putting her in the—these piece-of-shit wolves called it the waiting room, if you can believe that. Anyway, they started putting her in *that* room as punishment, once or twice a week. She's been in there for two months solid."

"Why?" Zach asked.

Alex shook his head. "They didn't know. Apparently Cage just said the girl would be living with them now. Tried to play it off like he was taking her in because she had nobody, but he didn't really care to give them any explanations, just expected them to be quiet and do what they were told. And they did." He swallowed his anger, looked away. "Nobody knows where she's from, just that Cage was gone for five days then showed up with her."

"Can we go?" Hillary asked Zach. "Go to a hotel?"

"I don't see why not. Myra will be a while here, but she doesn't need us. I'll ask her permission to take the girl...Alexis, home with us. I assume that's what you want?" She nodded and he left to make plans.

Stepping back into the guest bedroom, Hillary went to Stephen, putting her head on his shoulder while they watched Alexis sleep, guessing that this was the first easy sleep she'd been able to have in a long time.

When she felt Zach come back, she looked toward the door. He nodded. Hillary went to the sleeping child, brushed her hair back from her forehead.

"Alexis," she whispered.

The girl's eyes blinked then closed again.

"Alexis, we're going to get out of here. Go to a nice hotel, get a good breakfast. Okay?"

Again, the green eyes opened, her mouth twitched and she dropped back into sleep. Hillary reached down and scooped the small bundle into her arms, and walked out of the room. She took her to the car, and put her into the back, next to Theo, who buckled her in. She got into the driver's seat and waited for Zach to join them, and the rest of her wolves to get into the other car. When Zach got in, she started the car and drove away, feeling as though she was putting her nightmare behind her, once and for all, and driving forward toward her future.

CHAPTER THIRTEEN

A week later Hillary was still marveling at the girl's ability to adapt. She herself had required another good cry on Zach's shoulder to feel as if she were finally rid of the pain of her past. He'd held her so securely, so safely, she'd been astonished to see tears in his eyes too when she pulled back. He had made love to her so tenderly then, that she had cried just a little bit again, but in a completely different way. He had kissed those tears from her eyes as she came down from her climax, then powered into her until he reached his own, growling when she came again with him. That night she had run with her whole pack on the full moon for the first time, and the glorious feeling of belonging, of being loved and respected, had helped immensely.

Alexis had seemed happy to meet everyone, though slightly cautious. She stayed with Hillary and Zach the first night, but then she met Aaron and Tracy and fell immediately in love with two-year-old Ryder. When Tracy asked her if she would like to stay with them, the girl had responded with an actual smile. She had yet to say a single word, but was masterful at getting her wants and feelings across with just a look.

Like right now, when she clearly wanted to go with Todd, as he'd invited her to walk down the street with him to get an ice cream, but was reluctant to leave Hillary alone while she contemplated her shop and how best to dismantle it and move it to the site she'd picked in Mountain View. While she was excited about getting a bigger space and another helper, and the benefits of living there with the man she loved, far, far, far outweighed the negatives of moving, she was a little sad to see her first shop closing.

Hillary had finally broken down and told Zach exactly what she did and he'd given his support and encouragement while she decided on a new location. He seemed genuinely fascinated by her work and she couldn't wait for Aaron to give him his birthday present.

Squeezing the little hand gripped in hers, Hillary decided, "I could use an ice cream too. Can I come along?"

Alexis beamed and tugged Hillary and Todd out of the shop and down the street. They ate their ice cream and then headed back to the shop where Hillary met with the team who would be doing the packing and moving. She gave very specific instructions and left once she was satisfied that everything would be taken care of. They said goodbye to Todd and headed back to Mountain View.

Arriving at Aaron and Tracy's house, Hillary smiled to see Zach's SUV in the driveway. He hadn't been sure he would be able to make it for dinner. Alexis darted out of the car and met Zach on the porch where he waited with his arms held out. She launched herself at him, wrapping her skinny arms around his neck and giving him a rasberry on his cheek. He laughed and tickled her, then let her down to greet Ryder who squealed with delight when she came to pick him up.

They all trooped to the living room and Zach became serious. Alexis immediately picked up on the change in mood and set Ryder down next to his mother, then went to Zach, who put her in his lap. Her eyes were wide and a little bit wary, but not fearful.

"Alexis, our friend John has been working on finding your family. It took him a while, but he finally figured out you're from San Diego, California, right?" He looked at her gently, running his hand up and down her back as her breath hitched out. She gave a tiny nod. Aaron sat on the couch next to her and added his hand to his brother's. Hillary and Tracy knelt in front of them, each holding one of her hands. Ryder, not old enough to know what was going on, but old enough to be distressed to see his new favorite person sad, put his thumb in his mouth and leaned back in his mother's embrace.

Zach glanced around at everyone. "Alexis was taken from her home one night, after her parents were killed. The neighbors heard her screaming, but by the time they got there, she was gone." He watched Alexis' face carefully. "Did you see them? Did you see your parents?" The tears were falling freely now. Alexis shook her head slightly. "But you knew? You knew your parents were dead?" His voice was so gentle, but Hillary knew he was hurting, just as they all were, imagining what the little girl must have gone through. This time she nodded her head.

"Oh baby, you poor thing. I'm so sorry," Hillary said, reaching up to wipe at the tears.

Aaron cleared his throat, his voice hoarse. "Is there any other family?" Hillary could tell that he, like her, was conflicted. They wanted Alexis to have family that she could go to, but they didn't want her to leave.

"An aunt and uncle Alexis has never even met. A grandmother who's been in a nursing facility for years."

"Honey, would you like to stay here, with us? I'm so sorry your parents are gone, and I wish you had a big family that you could go home to, but I'm selfish and I hope you'll stay here, be part of our family, because we love you very much." Tracy was crying now too.

Alexis nodded then and they all breathed a sigh of relief.

"John said there's a wolf in Southern California, a lawyer, who can work on making this official and legal. He seems confident that if we throw enough money at the situation, it should go pretty smoothly." Zach kissed the top of Alexis' head and took a deep breath. "I'm starving, what's for dinner?"

They all went to the kitchen to get dinner on the table while

Alexis entertained Ryder in his highchair. When they had eaten, they watched Alexis' favorite DVD then put her and Ryder to bed. Zach told them that John Rodriguez had a lead on the male wolf who had been shot and escaped. They were hoping to track him down and make sure that he was okay. They had been in the living room less than an hour when the high-pitched scream had them running for the stairs.

"Mommy! Mommy, Daddy!" Alexis was sitting up in bed, her eyes wide in terror, screaming. Aaron grabbed her up, holding her tight to his chest, Tracy wrapping her arms around both of them, Hillary and Zachary flanking her. They whispered soothing words until the girl stopped shaking.

She laid her head on Aaron's shoulder and said, so quietly they could just make it out, "I don't want them to be dead. I miss them."

"I know you do, baby," Tracy told her. "And I know they miss you too. But they want you to be happy, they want you to live a good and happy life to make them proud."

Hillary took Zach's hand and pulled him out of the room and went to check on Ryder. He hadn't even woken up. Zach pulled Hillary into the hall and held her.

"Part of me wishes we'd kept her at our house. Made her ours," she whispered into his neck.

"I know, part of me wishes that too. But this is better for her, and we'll still be here for her. We did a good thing, made the right decision. She needs a family. Come on, let's go home."

They drove home in silence. When they walked into their house they went straight to the bedroom. Zach took her face in his hands, kissing her sweetly, gently. He moved his hands down and slowly unbuttoned her shirt, never breaking the kiss. She brought her hands up and did the same, slipping inside as soon as the shirt was open, loving the feel of him. She lightly scratched her nails down his back as he cupped her breasts. He growled, squeezing gently. She ran her hands over his back and chest, enjoying the way his muscles bunched as he unhooked her bra and pushed it out of his way.

Hillary wanted more. She ran her hands to his waistband,

pushing her fingers under his jeans, but didn't get far. She moved to the front and unbuckled his belt while he bent down enough to draw one nipple into his mouth. She gasped, her hands stilling as she concentrated on the delicious feelings. He switched to her other breast while his hands moved down to work her jeans open. This brought enough of her sanity back to remind Hillary that she was on a mission. She wanted to explore her man's body, and despite the fact they'd been having fabulous sex, she'd yet to get a chance before he turned her into a melted pile of mindless goo.

She opened his jeans enough to slide her hands beneath his underwear so she could cup his ass. It was a fine ass, enough flesh for her to grip him tightly. He mirrored her actions, but then he cheated. He brought one hand between her legs and gently swirled his finger through her creaming pussy. Hillary's breath hitched and Zach reclaimed her mouth, matching the tempo of his finger with that of his tongue. Her head fell back on a gasp, so he moved his mouth back to her breasts. Her own explorations were once again forgotten as he used his hands down below and his mouth moved back and forth between her breasts.

"Please, Zach, I need you," she managed between moans.

"You have me. You have all of me, forever."

"Inside me, please." The last word was a moan as her muscles clenched tight around his fingers.

"Later." He worked another finger into her despite her clutching and she went over. Her knees weakened as the orgasm rushed through her and Zach scooped her up and laid her back on the bed. He pulled her jeans all the way off, then his own. His hands gripped her ankles, then slowly smoothed up her legs, tickling behind her knees, kneading her thighs. He brought his face to her and inhaled deeply, a low growl almost like a purr, signaling his pleasure.

Her hands reached down and she threaded her fingers through his hair, needing to touch him. She gripped his hair tight when he swiped his tongue from bottom to top. His tongue pointed and stabbed at her clit and her hips jerked. He moved his hands to her hips to hold her steady for his assault. He nipped at her lips then thrust his tongue inside her as far as it would go. Lightning surged through her, taking her over the edge.

Zach kissed her clit gently then her bellybutton. He nipped at her ribs then sucked her nipples. By the time he got up to her mouth, Hillary was stirring again. Her hands reached out for him, grasping his biceps, nails biting into his muscles. He mated with her mouth as he drove into her. Her hips rocketed up to meet his thrusts. She brought her legs up, locking her ankles around his butt, pulling him into her as hard as she could. He put one strong arm under her pelvis, tilting her just right and she screamed as he hit the spot that made her toes curl. Finally he came and the feel of his seed shooting inside her brought on her final release.

Exhausted, Hillary rested in his arms, breathing hard, running her hands gently through his hair.

"You did it again," she said, wearily.

He grunted, but managed to make it sound questioning.

"You didn't let me have my turn." She pouted, though she was too tired to give it a good effort.

He gave her an affronted look. "I think you had three turns, if I was counting correctly."

She lightly smacked the back of his head. "That's not what I meant. You didn't give me a chance to explore your body. You keep promising but it never seems to happen."

He sighed. "I'm sorry, baby, it's the only way I can keep from coming. If you touched me like that, I wouldn't be able to hold off. Then what good would I be?"

She gave her own grunt in reply and drifted off to sleep.

THE NEXT DAY Zach and Hillary called Aaron and Tracy to find out how Alexis was. Tracy cried as she told them that Alexis was speaking, though not exactly a chatterbox.

They went over for breakfast and Hillary too had to force back the tears when Alexis shyly called her by name. She gave the girl a big hug.

"I'm so proud of you, sweetheart."

Zach stole the girl away and spun her around and around until she begged him to stop between peals of beautiful laughter. After breakfast they played outdoors for a while until they worked Ryder into exhaustion. When Tracy had put him down for his nap, Zach asked everyone to come into the living room.

"Alexis, you do know how glad we all are to have you here with us, don't you?" he asked the girl gently.

Alexis nodded her head shyly then looked up at him. "I know."

"When you're ready, I hope you'll be able to tell us what happened to you in Phoenix, so that we can help you deal with that. I know you met Claire and Tyler, but I don't know if you're aware that Claire is someone who helps people deal with difficult issues. It's her job to help people talk about things and feel better about them."

"She's very nice. She likes to help people." Alexis' voice was soft, barely more than a whisper, but sure.

"That's right. Maybe you could go talk to her next week. You don't have to talk about any particular thing until you're ready, but you've been through a lot of changes lately and it's probably a good idea to talk them through."

"Okay, Zach."

Zach glanced at Hillary, who nodded encouragingly.

"Honey," he said, taking Alexis' little hand into his much larger one. "Will you tell me what you know about the wolves?" Hillary could tell he was nervous, not sure what the girl would say, not sure how he could fix it if she became scared. She knew he also worried about the future, if she became angry with the pack for some reason and tried to hurt them with her knowledge.

Alexis' eyebrows drew down as she frowned. She opened her mouth and then closed it, clearly not sure what she was supposed to say.

Aaron reached over and lifted her chin in his hand, meeting her eyes with his own. "We love you, Alexis, you're part of us now. We just want to make sure that you're comfortable here and that we don't scare you."

She blinked, her frown deepening. "Some men are scary, and some women are scary, and some wolves are scary, but some people are nice and try to help. They feel happy when you're happy and sad when you're sad. And some wolves like to make you feel warm and safe." She ducked her head despite Aaron's hand. "I always know which are which. I can feel the difference." She seemed to be waiting for a reaction to that and Hillary had to fight back a laugh.

Alexis looked up, a tiny glare on her face, to meet the amusement of everyone else. It had clearly taken a lot of courage to admit this last bit and she didn't appreciate everyone finding it funny.

"Baby, we change into wolves. Did you think we would consider it weird to find a sweet little girl who knows what other people are feeling?" Tracy asked, wrapping her arm around the girl.

Alexis smiled and rolled her eyes, then sobered as the group became serious again.

"You need to help us understand this gift you have so that we don't accidentally make things harder for you. You understand?" Tracy asked.

Alexis seemed a little confused by the idea and Tracy and Hillary exchanged a look. Now that they knew the girl was empathic, not just sensitive, they would need to do some careful research to know best how to care for her. So far she hadn't seemed overwhelmed in any situation, but it would be best to be prepared. They would draw the details from her slowly though, since it was obvious she wasn't having difficulty at this point.

Hillary nodded at Zach and he brought the conversation back to where he'd started. "Alexis, did you know about werewolves before..." he grimaced, not sure of the best way to finish that.

She shook her head, her eyes wide. "I like animals and they almost always like me. Sometimes it's like I can talk to them, even though they aren't actually talking. I never knew some of them really could change into people and talk."

"Are you able to tell, just when you meet someone, that they have an animal inside too?"

Alexis nodded. "At first, I thought I was confused because they were bad people and I had never met such bad people before. Then a mean wolf came into my room one day and I knew it was the same bad man who took me from my mommy. Then I could tell the difference."

"Can you understand that most people don't know the difference?" Hillary asked. "And that they might be afraid? They don't know that there are good wolves and bad wolves and they might think that all wolves are bad and try to hurt them. So we don't tell regular people that we can be wolves too."

Alexis nodded and seemed to understand the point of the conversation. "I would never tell anyone, I swear."

Aaron hugged her tight. "We know, baby, we just need to make sure that you understand why you can't talk about it to strangers. We didn't know you could tell just by meeting someone if they were wolf too, or not. That's pretty impressive." He smiled proudly at her and she blushed.

"Mommy told me that not everyone could understand the animals so well, or what other people were feeling. She said people would be scared if they knew, so I had to try and keep it to myself most of the time. She said she was sorry about that, but that I could always come and tell her and Daddy about the animals. She was scared too when I started playing with the animals that aren't pets, but she said she trusted me to know which were good animals and which were bad." Her eyes grew sad.

Hillary wondered if this was behind Ken Cage's abduction of the girl. Could he have had some delusion that her abilities with animals could somehow be used to his advantage? She looked at Zach who met her eyes. It seemed he was thinking along the same lines.

"Sounds like you had a really good mommy and daddy. I know they must have been special, because they raised such a special little girl." Aaron kissed her cheek. "I hope you know you can come and tell us anything, anytime." He motioned to the four adults and she nodded.

Hillary stood up, pulling Zach with her. "What's for lunch, I'm starving?"

"Ice-cream sundaes!" came Alexis' suggestion. They all laughed and headed into the kitchen.

CHAPTER FOURTEEN

Zach cooked dinner for Hillary that night, claiming his steaks and baked potatoes were his best meal. She had to admit they were excellent. They sat in the living room for a while, talking about the pack, Alexis, her shop, his work. The conversation was easy and varied. Hillary sat on the couch with Zach's head in her lap, running her fingers through his hair as she loved to do.

"Let's go upstairs," she whispered, and Zach needed no further prompting. He got up and lifted her into his arms, carrying her up the stairs while peppering her face with gentle kisses. He sat her on the bed and took off his clothes while she watched hungrily. He growled when she licked her lips, and reached for her, but she slid off the bed and away from his reaching arms.

He growled again but stayed where he was when she held her hand out to him in a stopping gesture.

"What's the matter, baby?"

"Zach, I want you to do something for me." Her face was serious, but hopeful. He waited.

"I want you to let me touch you." He opened his mouth but she hurried on. "For real this time. You keep saying you'll let me but then you get going and either make me forget what I wanted or tell me not to so that you won't come. But I want to this time. I don't care if you climax, I want to feel you all over without *you* distracting *me*."

She watched his cock rise as she spoke but turned her pleading eyes on her mate. "Please?"

He groaned and flopped down onto the bed. "I'll try, Larry, I swear I will."

"Okay, Zach, that's all I ask." She took her jeans off but left her panties and shirt on. "Lie back on the bed," she instructed.

Zach gave her one long look then lay back, propping his head up on the pillow against the headboard. He rested his hands on his abdomen and waited.

Hillary swallowed hard, excited to finally have her chance. She got up on the bed and knelt by his feet. She picked up the foot farthest from her and examined it, running her fingers over the instep, slightly irritated that he wasn't ticklish. She pulled at his toes, laughing when they curled up on her. She set the foot down, farther away, then picked up his other foot, scooting herself in between his legs. She played with that foot for a moment, tracing a light scar on his heel then set it down as well.

Starting at his ankles, she slowly drew her hands up his legs, squeezing his calves, tickling his knees. When she reached his thighs, she bent down and kissed his knees, then licked the backs as he had done hers. His thighs tensed beneath her hands and she reveled in their strength. She bit gently on first one thigh then the other, pleased when his breathing picked up. She sat up and gave him a hard look, then bent down to his navel, being careful not to touch his penis.

She put her tongue into his bellybutton, laughing when his stomach muscles clenched. She kissed a trail up his middle while her hands explored his sides, which were heaving now. She took her mouth from him long enough to murmur, "Control, Zachary, you're a powerful werewolf. I know you have control." She bent back down and bit his knuckles, his hands having clenched into fists where they rested.

She sat up and took her shirt off, then scooted forward, once again being careful not to touch any of his private parts, then sat down on his stomach. She took his fists in her hands and kissed them, prying them open so she could kiss the palms. She set one arm down next to her thigh then examined the other. She sucked each finger into her mouth, smiling around them as he moaned. She felt his other hand fisting the sheets next to her leg and moved her mouth up to kiss the inside of his elbow then lick it.

She raised the hand above his head and worked her way back down it, kissing and nipping the tender flesh of his underarm. He was fighting to stay still now, and Hillary knew he would lose the battle soon if she didn't help him. She leaned over him, letting her breasts touch his mouth, while she searched under the pillow for the surprises she'd left there earlier. While Zach's mouth opened and sucked her nipple in, she took his wrist in one hand. She had to concentrate hard, trying to ignore the pleasure his mouth was bringing, feeling his other hand as it made its way up her side to her free breast, but she managed to clasp the handcuff around his wrist. Zach jerked, releasing her breast, surprise on his face. She sat back and looked at him.

She had already attached the other end of the cuff to the head-board and he craned his head around to see. He looked back at her, incredulous.

"Zach, sweetie. You're never going to stay still and let me have my wicked way with you if I don't help you out." She picked up his free hand and rested it on her thigh, caressing the wrist. Her intent was clear.

"Hillary..." He seemed unable to complete the thought.

"You trust me, don't you, Zach? It's not like I want to do anything crazy, it's just you won't let me touch you. Besides, it's not like you can't break them if you need to. I just want this one chance to play with your body. You said that I could."

He closed his eyes and heaved a deep breath. He gave a tiny nod but still flinched when she snapped the second cuff around his other wrist. She bent down and kissed both wrists, intentionally allowing her breasts to hang in front of his mouth. He took her offer and nuzzled between them before turning to one and biting gently. He growled when she sat back down on his stomach, though whether that was from being denied her breasts or because her panties were soaked completely through, she didn't care to guess.

Leaning down, she kissed him hard and he responded in kind. When she moved to draw back, he arched up, pulling her lower lip through his teeth. Hillary was panting hard now but she was determined to make this opportunity last. She ran her hands over his beautiful face, his cheekbones and eyebrows, giving them both a chance to calm down. She traced his mouth with her thumb and laughed when he drew it in. She pulled it free with a pop then traced it over his chin and down his neck. She leaned down to kiss the vulnerable spot, laving the hollow at his throat.

He ducked his chin, trying to move his mouth down to hers, but she continued on. She suckled on a nipple, pulling it gently with her lips, tickling it with her tongue, then switched to the other. When he drew up his thighs to squeeze her she bit the nipple, growling in warning until he yanked on the cuffs then lowered his legs again.

She got off the bed and hurried to the closet.

"Hillary." The warning was guttural but clear. She hurried back to the bed, two of her athletic socks in her hand. She fastened his ankles to the footboard, not looking at him, then climbed back onto the bed, resuming her initial position between his legs. His cock was stretched up conveniently, leaving her a clear view of his balls.

She fingered them gently then experimented, listening to his breathing and his moans to learn what he liked best. She leaned down and tasted him there, pleased when he jerked against all four of his bonds. She sat up again and lifted his straining penis into her hands. It was so hard and warm, she gasped at the feel of him.

"Baby, please." He was thrashing his head from side to side, sweat beading on his skin. Hillary moved to straddle one thigh while she played, so that she could press her clit against him. They both moaned at the contact, his leg jerking to bring her closer.

Returning her attention to what she held in her hands, Hillary leaned down, her warm breath causing him to twitch in her hands again. She ran her hands up his length, caught the bead of moisture waiting for her at the top, then back down again.

"Hillary, please. Let me go, I want to make you feel good."

"Oh Zach, trust me, I feel good." She ground herself down onto his leg so he could feel the truth of that.

"Shit, shit, shit." All his muscles were tense, and as she lowered her mouth to him he strained against her. "Seriously, Hillary, I won't last."

She laughed and sucked him into her mouth, hard. She went as far as she could then pulled back slowly. She took him all the way out, looked him in the eye and blew on his now-wet length.

"Fuck!"

"We'll get to that."

She returned to him and licked him this time, up one side then the other, then she concentrated on the head. She learned its shape, her hands holding him warm and steady. She put just the tip of him back in her mouth and sucked hard, her cheeks hollowing. With a bellow he came, and her throat worked hard to swallow him down. She smiled up at him, laughing at the weary expression on his face.

"Let me go, Larry, let me return the favor."

She laughed again. "You are so not getting this, Zach. You're mine, and I'm not done playing."

He glanced down at his emptied and limp cock and quirked his brow at her.

Ignoring him, she gently lifted him up and carefully licked his balls. The cock in her hand pulsed and she sat up with a smile. She kissed the crease where thigh meets groin, inhaling deeply. She sat up, moving forward so that she was kneeling up, straddling his stomach once again. Her eyes locked on his, she arched her back, bringing her hands up to lift her breasts as if in offering. Zach jerked his hands against the cuffs, then narrowed his eyes at her and lay back down.

She ran her hands down her torso and waist to the sides of her hips. She had bought these panties special, because they tied at the side. She knew Zach hadn't noticed before, but he was noticing now. She untied each side then pulled them out in front of her, laying them on Zach's chest where he could smell her arousal more easily. She sat down, her swollen lips wet against his stomach. She glanced over her shoulder to confirm that life was returning to that now-neglected organ.

She bent over him, once again reaching under the pillow. She pulled her hand back, careful not to let him see what she held.

"I have another present for you," she said.

Zach groaned. "Oh shit, what now?"

She smiled and opened her hand, letting the nipple clamps fall to his stomach.

"Oh fuck, baby."

Hillary kept her eyes on his face while she caressed her breasts.

"Do you think you could get them nice and hard for me, Zach?"

"Yeah, baby. I'm pretty sure I could do that for you, if you bring them down here." He looked like a man starving.

She put her hands on either side of his head and leaned over, swinging first one nipple, then the other, closer and closer to his mouth. He growled and reared up to capture one. She gasped, giving in, letting him lower his head, his prize caught. He worked her carefully, faithfully, completely, until she was gasping. Then he released her with a gentle pop and waited patiently for her to give him her other breast. She didn't even pause. Finally, she pulled back, and he let her go with a little pull from his teeth.

She reached down and picked up one of the clamps, then put it on fast. She gasped at the momentary pain then attached the second one. Zach's eyes were glued to her nipples and the little beaded clamps dangling down, connected by a silver strand. The chain dangled freely between her breasts, hypnotizing. He licked his lips.

Squeezing his sides with her thighs, she worked her clit against his stomach, her hand returning to play with her now-tender breasts. She pulled gently on the chain and gasped. Zach mirrored it with a gasp of his own. He was growling continuously now, his hips rocking up to try to find her.

Hillary rose up on her knees again and swung around to face the other way. She saw that he was erect again, if not quite as fully as before. She smiled and placed her hands on either side of his hips, arching her back to give him the best view, lowering her torso so that he could see the jewelry dangling from her chest, between her legs.

"Fuuuuck," he moaned.

Hillary leaned down to lick him some more, pleased when his hips thrust up to meet her eager mouth. She rewarded him by reaching one hand down to slip inside her pussy. The cock in front of her jerked each time her fingers disappeared inside. She gathered her cream onto her fingers and brought it to his cock. He shuddered when she used her own wetness to lubricate him. She went back for more then moved up his body. Using her hand to hold him steady, she slowly lowered herself down onto him.

"Aargh," Zach gurgled. She rose and fell, rose and fell, swiveling her hips to make it more interesting. When she knew she was close, she came all the way down and was still. She brought her finger, still wet with her cream, in front of her, bent over, and rested it against his puckered hole. Zach's whole body stiffened further and she looked back at him.

"They say that there are a lot of nerve endings here," she said. "If it hurts, just tell me and I'll stop."

"Oh fuck," was all he managed at hearing his own words repeated back to him. He closed his eyes and gave her a tiny nod. Hillary rotated her hips and thrust the finger home. He shuddered.

"Zach, there's one more thing I bought at the store." She watched him drag his eyes open as she reached under the blanket for the last item. She'd thought the butt plug was the same size as the one he'd bought for her, but when she'd brought it home it had turned out to be smaller. But then, he didn't have to prepare for a cock, so it should do. He stared at the bright blue plug, then at her.

He sighed. "Whatever you want, baby. I made you wait long enough."

She gave him a huge grin then faced forward again, lifting her rear to give him a nice view of his cock disappearing between her folds. She had to reach for the lube where she'd stashed it, and he bucked when her muscles squeezed him tight automatically. She hurried back into position, not knowing how much more time she had. She squeezed lube onto the plug until it was dripping then eased it to his pucker.

"Ready, baby?" she asked him, already giving a tiny push.

"Fuck." His hips rose, thrusting his cock into her harder and pushing his asshole against the toy which entered smoothly to the first knuckle.

She turned to check on him. He was sweating and gripping the chains of the cuffs. Twisting back around, she used her connection to him, instead of her eyes, and found nothing but pleasure and excitement. Thrilled, she pushed harder on the plug and seated it to the second knuckle and then the third. She pulled herself off him and he pulled hard on the chains, causing the metal to creak.

"Larry!"

"It's okay, Zach, I'm just turning around." She did as promised, lowering back over him until she was as far down as she could go. Then she leaned over him until the chain between her nipples dangled in front of his mouth. He opened wide and took the chain in his teeth, arching his head so that they could watch each other.

One careful breath, then she nodded. He pulled on the chain at the same time she sat up, popping the clamps off. Sensation shot through her entire body and she came at once with a long scream. Zach shouted and bucked up into her as he, too, came. She reached behind her and carefully pulled out the plug, earning a long moan from him.

She was totally spent, but rather than collapsing over him like she wanted to, she dragged herself off him and staggered from the bed to the bathroom. Washing her hands, she wet a washcloth with warm water. Returning to him, she wiped him clean then untied his ankles. She threw the washcloth into the bathroom, hoping she hit the sink but not much caring at this point.

She got the keys to the handcuffs from the drawer beside the bed and climbed back up, reaching to release him. She tried to massage his shoulders but he wrapped his arms tight around her and they both fell asleep.

SIX DAYS LATER, they were back in Slade. Zachary and Hillary stood in front of the mayor, their friends and family arrayed behind them. She wore a creamy dress, long and flowing, and he wore a charcoal suit. The ceremony itself was short, followed by a reception at the Italian restaurant in town. They'd rented it out for the night, using a side area near the bar for a dance floor. They had a small orchestra set up and the leader called out for Zach and Hillary to come take their first dance.

Hillary realized she'd never danced with her man before. She'd known him less than a month, but he was firmly lodged in her heart and soul and she couldn't remember how she was ever happy without him in her life. They danced slowly, eyes locked on each other. She brought one hand up to the nape of his neck, teasing his hair. She loved to feel the silk of it sliding through her fingers. On impulse, she gave it a slight tug.

"Mine," she whispered.

He brought his hands up to cup her face, pulling her in gently. "Mine," he whispered, and kissed her.

EXCERPT

Challenge Accepted
(Wolf Appeal Book 2)
By KB Alan
(Now available)

Since being turned into a werewolf, Adam has been a loner. Practically a hermit. Okay, actually a hermit. When the local wolves and werewolves start experiencing weird behavior, he can't resist the pull to step up and see if he can help. And runs smack into trouble in the form of the werewolves' National President.

Myra's term as President is nearly over, but she's determined to track down the wolf who was attacked, and turned against his will. When she meets Adam, she only wants to help him live a full and happy life. Then she sees him naked. And gets to know him. And decides she wants a lot more for him than to just escape his lonely cabin in the woods.

CHAPTER ONE

The forest was his, and he no longer questioned it. Other wolves, natural wolves, roamed the same land, but they didn't bother him. They acknowledged his place in their territory and both sides were content to leave the other alone.

Adam paced the tree line to the north of his cabin, uneasy. Something was off in his territory and he needed to figure out what it was. He'd run across two seemingly rabid wolves, one the week before, the other just yesterday, that he'd had to put down. He'd felt sick doing it, but there'd been no choice. He couldn't risk the wolves making the others sick or getting too close to town. The farmers in the area already disliked the wolves, were pushing to have their protected status revoked and hunting season declared once again.

Adam had checked the werewolf database and forum—and wasn't it a kick in the pants that such a thing even existed—and managed to find out that the nearby werewolf pack, headquartered about thirty miles away, had also experienced something similar. Only, their incident hadn't been a natural wolf, but a sick werewolf who'd attacked its own pack members.

Adam shook himself in irritation, resettled his fur and headed back to the cabin. The information he'd seen online about the local pack's experience was sketchy. A young member had come out of the woods fighting, and it had taken a much stronger wolf than necessary to put her into submission. She'd finally gone unconscious, with a high fever, and when she woke, hardly remembered a thing. The worry, of course, other than not understanding what was making her and the natural wolves sick, was that if a stronger wolf were to be affected, they might cause real damage before someone powerful enough could stop them.

More worrisome was word from the town. There'd been talk about the rabid wolves, even though the local vet had stated that no rabies had been found. Talk about getting some hunters together to take care of the problem if the local officials weren't going to handle it. Adam wasn't sure which idea was worse, local hunters invading his land, firing willy-nilly, or the government coming in thinking they could do whatever it was government employees thought they should do to handle the situation.

He had to consider the possibility that the pack had more information than had been posted online, and if he didn't figure out what was going on, he was going to have to talk to them. Which irritated the hell out of him.

Pulling his human form to the front, he let the wolf fall away and strode into his cabin. He stepped into sweatpants and moved to the kitchen area.

A quick jiggle of his old teapot confirmed there was plenty of water in it and he turned on the stove. He pulled his not-so-old coffee press out of the cupboard and went through the mindless steps of producing coffee while he mulled over the problem. If the townspeople thought there was an outbreak of rabies, even though he was pretty sure that wasn't what was happening, they could go on the offensive. The last thing he needed was human hunters invading his property, firing at anything that looked like a wolf, including himself. Been there, done that, no need to repeat the experience, thank you very much.

When the coffee was ready, he moved to the couch and sipped thoughtfully. The first taste was perfect, and he smiled. He may live with very few of the trappings of civilization, but no way was he giving up good coffee.

Not getting shot again was also a priority, but so was keeping humans and werewolves out of his territory, just for his own peace of mind. Getting kidnapped, tortured and turned into a werewolf had just been a bit more than his already somewhat introverted nature could stand, and he'd given up on wanting anything to do with people.

When he'd found and hacked into the werewolf site, he'd searched for stories like his, but come up blank. Apparently the crazy-as-fuck pack that had kidnapped, tortured and turned him had been the exception, not the rule.

Still, even after he'd come to that conclusion he hadn't been much interested in meeting up with others of his kind. He'd roamed the states for a couple of years until he'd hit on this part of Montana. Close enough to the pack that he could pretty much identify, and therefore avoid, where they lived and worked, but far enough away that he didn't have to work too hard to remain unknown.

He didn't remember a lot from that week six years ago. He recalled being invited out to a ranch by Paula Cage and enjoying a lovely barbecue before her crazy-ass brother had turned into a werewolf—an honest-to-god fucking werewolf!—and attacked him.

After that, things got hazy, though he still had uncomfortable flashes of Paula trying to get him to have sex with her while he was bleeding and only half-conscious. Fucking nuts, all of them. When the full moon had risen the next night, and he'd turned into a wolf himself, he'd taken off. Which was when the fuckers had shot him.

The whole thing still struck him as completely bizarre, even after all these years. He'd eventually come to realize that the pack he'd first encountered wasn't the norm, and he'd discovered there were plenty of werewolves out there who were normal, law-abiding citizens, but that didn't mean he had any desire to socialize with them, any more than he was willing to hang out with humans and risk being found out. Or risk hurting them; losing control somehow and turning them by mistake.

He finished his coffee and contemplated the teetering stack of books by the couch. It was almost time to make a trip into town, drop off the books he'd read, pick up some new ones, as well as other supplies. If he waited too long, it was a pain in the ass to haul the larger quantity of books to and from the old pickup he kept on the east side of his land. He divided up his trips, hitting the town that was closer to pack land only a couple of times a year, and interspersing that with trips to the other side of the mountain.

So far, he'd managed to avoid running into any of the pack while in town, and as far as he knew, they weren't aware he existed. He'd learned enough about their ways to figure he'd be able to talk himself clear of any situation, mostly due to the fact that he wasn't breaking any of their laws, other than remaining anonymous. Technically, he was supposed to let the Bitterroot hierarchy know he was there so they could make sure he was following said laws, but what they didn't know wouldn't hurt him. He'd been in the area three years with no contact and until now he'd seen no reason to change that.

With a sigh at the idea that it might finally be time to come out of the werewolf closet, he moved to turn on the generator, get some hot water going. He'd make dinner, run a load of laundry, wash the dishes, and take a nice hot shower before going to bed, sleeping on the problem.

Just before flipping the switch, he frowned at the distant buzzing sound coming from outside. It wasn't often he heard low-flying planes in the area, but it seemed like lately it had been more frequent.

He turned on the generator and grabbed a sweatshirt on his way to the front door, having cooled off from his earlier run.

The sun had set and the light was nearly gone, but he could just pick out the plane a couple of miles to the west, heading toward town. Something else to look into, he figured, though he wasn't sure where to start on that. Maybe he could hack into the local airport, see if it was possible to identify the plane that way. He made note of the time and went back inside to make his dinner. If he didn't have any brilliant ideas before morning, he was going to have to suck it up and do what needed to be done.

Two days later

The vast expanse of forest called to Myra, beautiful in twilight. She wished she could shuck her clothes, her shoes, those trappings of civilization that usually grounded her, stand naked in the cool mountain air for just a minute, before allowing the fur and simplicity of her wolf to overtake her. The wind whistled softly through the branches, birds called out cheerfully to each other, and the crisp, clean smells vouched for the two-hour drive out of the city.

Sighing, she turned her back on the enticing sight and faced the wolves who'd come out of the pack house to greet her.

She could feel their nervousness, should do something to calm their worries, but was too on edge herself. They'd called in to the National Council to report a problem but hadn't expected her, the current National President, to show up. What they didn't know was that their problem seemed to be coinciding with *her* problem, one she wanted to clear up as soon as possible. Needed to clear up.

Not that she could just fix it. That was the real tragedy. No matter what she did, what the pack did, there was no fixing this. An innocent man had been brutally attacked, turned into what he would surely perceive to be a monster, then escaped to live the life of a werewolf without the support of those like him.

If they'd found him, like she believed, she could offer that support now, answer any questions he might still have after all these years, let him know that the evil shits responsible for his attack had been taken care of. But she couldn't fix it. Couldn't give him back the life he'd lost.

The alpha pair gave her a slight bow and she nodded and managed a distracted smile before preceding them inside. She'd known Michael and Linda for years, but they weren't particularly friends. All reports she'd studied while flying north to meet them indicated that Bitterroot was a healthy pack, not very large considering the vastness of land available in Montana, but tight knit and happy.

They settled into seats and the pair waited for her to begin while Simone, the third in their pack hierarchy, brought in a plate of refreshments. Myra thanked her, accepted a cup of tea and took a sip, waiting for Michael and Linda to take their drinks as well.

"Linda," she began. "After you spoke to Tom about what had happened down here, he called me, as I may have a particular interest in part of your story. Would you mind going over what you told him, giving me the details directly?"

Tom, the current National Secretary and therefore main point of contact between the packs and the head organization, had called her as soon as he'd hung up with the Bitterroot alpha. He would have done that anyway, due to the problem with pack was having, but he'd also been excited to share the news about the unknown wolf.

"Of course. It started a few weeks back. One of the pack ran across a wolf that was acting sick. We thought rabies at the time. She had to put the poor thing down, and brought the body back." She glanced nervously at her husband.

"We considered destroying the body," Michael said, his back straightening.

Myra knew if he'd been in wolf form she'd see his hackles rising.

"But if there really was a rabies outbreak happening, the town needed to know."

She nodded her agreement and the couple's tension level eased down several notches.

"Animal control said they didn't actually find rabies, had some odd test results but couldn't say anything definitive," Linda continued. "He wouldn't confirm poison or drugs, said he needed to run more tests. We put the word out to the pack to be on the lookout for any other odd wolf behavior, and not to eat anything they weren't sure of, for fear of poison, but nothing happened for another week."

"Except," Michael jumped in, "the vet received another dead wolf, which he also confirmed was rabies-free."

"But we didn't know that at the time," Linda finished. "What happened next was one of our own wolves got sick. A few of the teens had gone out for a run, and this one, Denny, came back on his own, acting wildly out of control, completely unlike himself. Our first was able to subdue him until Michael showed up."

"He was sick, running a high fever, sweating, breathing hard." Michael stood and began to pace. "They said before Jake was able to calm him down he'd been attacking whoever came near, even our third." He gestured to where Simone had left the room. "Which is crazy, he's nowhere near strong enough to challenge a member of the hierarchy. Once I got there he was able to calm down even more and went to sleep for about twelve hours. When he woke up he barely remembered any of it, thought it had been a nightmare, or a fever-induced hallucination."

"Jake was the first to comment on the similarity to the sick wolf," Linda added.

Michael sat back down, took his mate's hand in his. "The next night, another of my wolves, a sixteen-year-old who I think will likely be hierarchy one day, turned up the same way. Out of her head, threatening anyone who came near. When I got there, I could tell that she was just barely hanging on to her control. Actually, once she realized I was there, she lost her control and attacked. We had to hold her down so I could force her submission. Once she submitted, it was just like it had been with Denny. Liv was sick, she slept, she barely remembers."

Shaken by the story, Myra considered. She'd never heard of such a thing. "Would you know if natural wolves up here were acting rabid?" Myra asked.

"Yes. No question. There are enough hunters, ranchers and farmers in the area who hate that the wolves are protected. They would jump on any excuse to have that protection stopped. It's why we hesitated before going to animal control, but if there really had been an outbreak of something..."

Myra nodded. Some areas of the country had a much more delicate balance with the hunters and local population than others. "And then you met the lone wolf."

Michael glanced at his wife but she motioned for him to continue the story. "He showed up in town yesterday, walked up to one of our wolves and asked her for her alpha's phone number, or for her to call and give us his number. Linda and I went right out to meet him. Said his name was Adam and he lived not too far away."

"Wouldn't say where, exactly," Linda interjected.

"Wouldn't say where," Michael confirmed, "but said he had some acres and kept to himself, but he was concerned about the sick wolves. Said he'd heard we'd had a couple of sick kids, as well, and wanted to see if we had any new info to share."

"I'd like to know how he knew about the kids," Linda said, the anger in her voice clear. "It's not like it's something we were talking about freely."

"You guys didn't like him," Myra said.

Michael winced.

"He wasn't..." Now Linda hesitated. "He knew he was expected to let us know he was living here, he wasn't ignorant of the rules, he just didn't care. Blatantly."

Michael nodded. "But on the other hand, whether it seems like it right now or not, Linda and I, our hierarchy, we have a good handle on our region. We may not have known he was there, but we for sure would have known had he been making any trouble."

Linda pursed her lips. "I didn't like him, you're right. Doesn't sit well with me that he's out there all by himself, avoiding us for years. It's not natural. It's not wolf." She sighed. "But, I did believe him that he's been behaving himself, and that he's trying to help figure out this problem." She glanced at her husband, got a nod from him. "The other thing is, well...he's stronger than us. And it's *really* not natural for a wolf that alpha to not want to be pack. So, what's he doing out here, all by himself?"

Myra debated how much to tell the alpha pair. Ultimately, the matter couldn't be swept under the rug. Pretending it hadn't happened wouldn't make sure it never happened again. "I got a call a couple of weeks ago from Mountain Pack, in Idaho. Seems their alpha found his mate, a woman named Hillary. She told him that she'd been attacked and turned, four years ago."

Linda gave off a gasp and Michael gaped at her.

"I know. It gets worse. An entire rogue pack had formed in Phoenix, Arizona. Led by a man named Ken Cage, who was related to the alpha pair in the Mesa pack." She took a deep breath, trying to calm the anger that burned even now, weeks after bringing those wolves to justice. "Cage liked to find humans and convince his pack that they could be turned. Then attack them, and if they were female, which they mostly were, rape them, until they died."

Linda looked physically ill and Michael looked confused. "That doesn't make any sense, that's not how wolves are turned. Besides, anyone strong enough to live through that isn't going to stick around with the idiots who turned him."

"Exactly. So, not only was Cage a crazy bastard, he was also an idiot. And you're right, both wolves who survived escaped once they turned. The others didn't survive. To add insult to injury, the bastard couldn't even remember his victim's name."

"And you think this Adam is the other wolf that did?" Linda asked.

"I hope he is. Cage says he shot the teacher that turned, but never found a body. Which doesn't mean he really got away, of course. But I'm hoping." If their Adam really was just a lone wolf, one who, for whatever reason, shirked the need for contact, companionship, and touch that most wolves craved, that was fine. But she needed to find her missing wolf, do whatever was possible to help him understand the world he'd been forced into, be as at peace as possible with the wolf within himself. Of course, there was always the chance that the teacher had died, but she would exhaust all possible efforts before giving up.

"That's just awful," Linda said. "To have lived all this time alone, no pack, no family, just…" She shook her head. Michael took her hand, his thumb gliding an absent pattern over her skin. For the first time in a long time Myra felt a pang of longing for her mate. It had been more than fifteen years since Eric had been killed. Wolves touched a lot, so it wasn't like she didn't have physical contact on a regular basis, but it wasn't the same.

She shook her head and returned her attention to the couple. Wolves were pack animals. They needed to touch, smell, be with each other. The fact that Adam wanted nothing to do with them wasn't a good sign, but at least he'd come forward to help with the sick wolves. She focused on that.

"I know. I need to talk to him, find out if he's the same wolf. If he's not, I'll still help with the current situation while I continue to search for the teacher. If he is, I'm hoping we can figure something out to help him integrate, or adjust, or…whatever we can do." She paused, took a sip of her nearly forgotten tea. "He's stronger than you? Even as a pair?"

Michael nodded his confirmation. "Definitely."

"Then hopefully he really is the one I'm looking for. It would take a very strong wolf to survive what he did." She was anxious to meet him, to know for sure. "How did you leave it with him."

"He gave me a cell phone number, took mine. Said he'd call if he found anything out, asked me to do the same. He was polite, didn't try and push any power or anything. I'm sure he knew we were irritated, but he stayed cool."

"I have no reason to believe that you don't have an excellent handle on this territory. If he'd been misbehaving in anyway, I'm sure it would have come to your attention before now."

They nodded, looking relieved. Michael pulled out his phone. "Would you like me to call him?"

"Yes, please. Ask him to meet us tomorrow, somewhere he won't feel threatened. I'll trust you to pick a suitable location."

Find purchase links for Challenge Accepted at
www.kbalan.com/books/challenge-accepted

To join KB Alan's newsletter, visit www.kbalan.com/newsletter

ALSO BY KB ALAN

Perfect Fit Series (Erotic Romance)

Perfect Formation (Book 1)

Perfect Alignment (Book 2)

Perfect Stranger (Book 2.5)

Perfect Addition (Book 3)

Perfect Temptation (Book 4)

Fully Invested (Contemporary Romance)

(Part of the Wildlife Ridge World)

Coming Home (Book 1)

Breaking Free (Book 2)

Finding Forever (Book 3)

Wolf Appeal Series (Paranormal Romance)

Alpha Turned (Book 1)

Challenge Accepted (Book 2)

Going Deeper (Book 3)

Stand Alone

Bound by Sunlight (Erotic Romance)

Keeping Claire (Fantasy Romance)

Sweetest Seduction (Contemporary Romance)

www.kbalan.com

ABOUT THE AUTHOR

KB Alan lives the single life in Southern California. She acknowledges that she should probably turn off the computer and leave the house once in a while in order to find her own happily ever after, but for now she's content to delude herself with the theory that Mr. Right is bound to come knocking at her door through no real effort of her own. Please refrain from pointing out the many flaws in this system. Other comments, however, are happily received.

www.kbalan.com

To join KB's newsletter, visit www.kbalan.com/newsletter

f facebook.com/kbalan
🐦 twitter.com/KB_Alan
📷 instagram.com/authorkbalan
BB bookbub.com/authors/kb-alan

Printed in the USA
CPSIA information can be obtained
at www.ICGtesting.com
LVHW012245220823
756018LV00032B/779